MRS. THISTLETHWAITE AND THE MAGPIE

ALSO BY J. B. HAWKER

The First Ladies Club Series

The First Ladies Club
A Body in the Belfry
A Corpse in the Chapel

The Bunny Elder Novels

Hollow
Vain Pursuits
Seadrift
...and Something Blue

Short Story Collections

Cozy Christmas Sweets
Cozy Campfire Shorts

MRS. THISTLETHWAITE AND THE MAGPIE

A Tillamook Tillie Mystery

J. B. Hawker

Copyright © 2017 J.B Hawker

ISBN-13:978-1545370384
ISBN-10:1545370389

Dedicated to my family

and my

Very Important Readers

For their encouragement and support.

1

All eyes in the grand concert hall followed the movements of the lithe *prima ballerina assoluta.* Her audience sighed as she whirled on the stage. With her graceful limbs extended in fluid movements, she plucked the emotions of her audience in a story without words.

Music surged from the orchestra, lifting her on its strains as she seemed to float above the floor.

Dressed in their finest evening wear, the enraptured watchers held their breath as this lyrical vision twirled, leaped, and soared ever higher...

"Aargh!"

"Oops! Sorry Honora," a chubby teen in a black leotard said, reaching a hand to help her classmate to her feet. "Are you okay?"

Honora Anniston, jerked from her fantasy by the younger girl's awkward misstep, smiled up at her.

"Not your fault, Sarah. I wasn't watching, either. I was sort of carried away with the music," she said rolling her eyes, then grimacing as she stood up.

"You're not hurt, are you?" Sarah asked.

"Nah. Just tweaked my ankle a little. It will be fine."

"Ladies! Ladies!" their teacher called out. "Let's take it from the top."

*

Outside the Twinkle Toes Dance Studio, fog rolling up Tillamook Bay began to coat the trees and shrubs with mist.

In the fading daylight, a dark figure skulked in the tall roadside weeds. He shifted to relieve his cramping muscles and made a sound of disgust when he felt dampness seeping through the knees of his trousers.

"Come on, come on," he breathed.

For weeks, he'd dreamed of this day. His senses quivered in anticipation as he focused on the

2

studio at the end of the small town's strip mall. Neighboring businesses were already closed. The area deserted, except for a few cars in the studio's gravel parking lot.

*

"Timing, ladies! Keep together, one-two!" Mimsy Waits shouted to her class of awkward young dancers as they leaped and twirled inside the squat cinder block building.

"Posture, posture!" she cried, clapping her chubby hands. "Okay, take a break!"

"Miss Waits, can we do that last section, again? I almost got it this time," willowy blond Honora, begged.

"Take your break, first. You gotta keep hydrated," Mimsy replied. "Besides, you've got it down, already. Your solo is going to be a show-stopper at the hospice benefit show."

The mirrored wall reflected ten teenage dancers in identical black leotards slumped against the barre drinking from water bottles and wiping away sweat.

"Miss Waits!" a tiny dancer, barely in her teens, called out. "Are we about done? My mom just texted me. She's waiting for me out in the parking lot."

Mimsy looked at the large round wall clock, checked her watch, and sighed.

"I guess we'd better call it a night, girls. But, keep practicing at home. Our performance is only three weeks away. You're getting close, but you're not ready, yet," she said. "Tell your mom I'm sorry I kept you so late, Emily!"

*

Concealed in the brush nearby, the watcher pictured every detail of the sinister delights to come. The girl would be surprised and scared, of course. But, she'd soon calm down. He'd been fantasizing and making careful preparations ever since the day he'd seen her fly past on her bicycle with her golden hair streaming in the wind. He knew she was the special one he'd been waiting for.

4

Tonight, everything was ready; there was no more reason to delay.

"Come on, come on! Hurry up!" he growled under his breath.

As if in response, the door he'd been watching opened and laughing and chattering young girls emerged from the building.

*

Inside, Honora gathered up her things, put on her jacket, and slung her backpack over one shoulder. As she walked toward the exit, her friends, Samantha and Shantee, joined her.

"You were awesome on the arabesque, Honora!" Shantee said. "How do you keep your balance like you do?"

"Yeah, you're gonna be amazing at the charity performance," Samantha added.

"Thanks, guys. You're doing really good, too," Honora said. "I still need to work on the ballonné, though. My ankle was hurting tonight, so I was kinda wobbly on the landing."

"Tell me about it!" Shantee said. "My feet are killing me. Old Lotsa Weight kept us too late."

"It's easy for her, just sitting on her fat backside on a stool, stuffing her face with energy bars, while we kill ourselves for hours trying to please her," Samantha agreed.

"Don't be mean!" Honora said. "Miss Waits probably can't help being a little chubby. I'll bet her metabolism got all messed up when she was a professional dancer in New York City. Can you imagine what that life must have been like? I'd give anything to get a shot with one of the New York dance companies."

"You're good enough. You should send audition tapes," Samantha said.

"Nah. My folks would never let me go clear across the country. Mom's always reminding me how I'm her only chick and she wants to keep me in the nest as long as possible," Honora said, mimicking her mother's voice with a grin and rolling her eyes.

"I'll be too old by the time I'm on my own, anyway. I turn seventeen next week, so it's almost too late to try to go pro. Maybe I'll be a dance teacher, like Miss Waits.," she added with a shrug.

"Not like her! No way," Samantha laughed.

Shantee waved at her big brother, James, who'd pulled his car into the parking lot as they emerged from the studio.

"You want a ride, Honora? It's getting kinda dark," Shantee offered, walking over to the car.

"No, thanks. I've got my bike. I'll take the shortcut through the park and be home before it gets too late. See you tomorrow!"

James honked to hurry up his passengers and Honora peddled off into the gathering darkness with a wave,

She passed under a street light and the watcher became an active predator. He jogged along the verge to keep pace with his prey, staying in the shadows until the perfect moment to strike. His heart pounded and his breathing was rapid as he closed the gap between them.

Honora switched on the headlamp mounted between the bike's handlebars. The sun was down, although it wasn't fully dark, yet, and she wanted traffic to be able to see her in the light fog.

Her parents reminded her almost every time she took her bike out that twilight was the most dangerous time for a cyclist. While she might sometimes resent their protectiveness, she seldom ignored their advice.

They'd wanted to keep chauffeuring her everywhere, but she was too old to be carted around like a preschooler, so this year she'd put her foot down. She knew better than to ask to get her driver's license, though.

Honora smiled as she pedaled, thinking how lucky she was to have two parents who loved her enough to be overly protective. Lots of her friends' parents couldn't care less.

She usually cycled the three miles from the dance studio to her home in bright daylight. The gathering darkness made this familiar road seem strange and ominous, somehow, and the fog-muffled sounds added a feeling of isolation.

A low curb separated the road from the path through the woods

Honora shook off her unease and stood on the pedals, wincing when she put weight on her sore ankle as she bumped the bike over. She settled back down onto the bicycle seat, wondering what her mom would have on the table for dinner. She was famished, as usual.

The mist grew thicker once she crossed into the park. The odors of salt water and decay from the nearby slough grew stronger and Honora pedaled faster.

She heard the rustling of nocturnal animals foraging in the undergrowth and tried to ignore a growing sensation of being watched. Skirting the wooded wilderness area, her anxiety grew.

She was starting to regret her decision to ride home through the park when a branch snapped behind her. It was followed by heavy footsteps pounding on the pavement, and she was pulled roughly to the ground.

Before she could cry out, something was pressed over her nose and mouth and a sweet odor overwhelmed her senses.

Honora and her attacker disappeared into the trees, leaving her bicycle sprawled on its side with the wheels slowly spinning on the empty path.

2

Early morning mist rose from the park foliage as forty-year-old Marcia Wildmon, dressed in stylish exercise gear, jogged along the bike path, keeping time with the music coming from her headphones. From time to time, she glanced at the sports band on her wrist, checking her heart rate.

Rounding a corner, she almost stumbled over a bicycle lying across the path. She swore under her breath, but quickly recovered her regular rhythm, putting the near-accident out of her mind.

After Marcia passed, a vagrant scrounging for recyclables emerged from the bushes. He saw the abandoned bicycle, picked it up and, after looking around to see if anyone was looking, hopped on and pedaled away, congratulating himself on his good luck.

*

Later that morning at the Tillamook Senior Center, Tillie's Ripe and Ready Yoga Class was in full swing. Elderly women togged out in their own unique interpretations of appropriate yoga wear were seated on mats, struggling with varying degrees of success to follow the movements of their equally mature, but still energetic leader.

"Inhale, sit up straight, now exhale while placing your right hand on your left knee...your left knee, Edna, that's it... now, lengthen your spine and look over your right shoulder, turning your head as far as you... oh, forevermore! What's that racket?"

Matilda Thistlethwaite stopped mid-instruction when the discordant strains of what sounded like either The Battle Hymn of the Republic, The Colonel Bogey March, or The Yellow Rose of Texas, filled the air and the center's multi-use room was invaded by a ragtag marching band holding kazoos to their lips.

A gaggle of enthusiastic and musically

challenged senior citizens followed their high-stepping leader into the room, circling the startled yoga class.

The tall, lanky director waved his long arms like a symphony conductor and his thick, slightly too-long silver hair flopped in time with the marching feet until he lifted a whistle to his lips and blew a shrill blast, bringing his wobbly followers to a stuttering halt.

In the blessed quietness which followed, he turned toward Matilda with a broad grin.

"Well, Tillie, what do you think? Are we ready for prime time?"

"Slim Bottoms! What's the idea of interrupting our yoga class like this?" Tillie asked with her hands on her well-padded hips.

Standing a compact five-foot-nothing in a yoga costume of bright yellow leggings topped by a flowing multi-colored tunic, with her long white hair in a single braid flung over one shoulder, Slim thought she resembled an exotic, angry dumpling.

"Ah, heck! We just wanted to show you our new band, Tillie. Don't be mad," Slim said, looking down at her and trying not to smile.

"Yoga is a peaceful exercise, Slim! Relieving stress helps us keep our memories sharp. We need quiet to relax and allow our muscles to become flexible, too. Being ambushed by your cacophony is hardly conducive," she said.

"Ambushed? By us?" Slim exclaimed, sweeping his arms wide to include his group. "I'll have you know we are the newly formed, soon-to-be-renowned, musical group of Slim Bottoms and the Wrinkly Keesters Kazoo Band, and I won't have you calling us a caco-whatsit."

Tillie burst out laughing in spite of herself, and the yoga students and kazoo players, who had been silently observing this encounter, joined in.

"I guess that will be all for today, class," Tillie called over the ensuing laughter and lively conversations.

"Slim, you are a caution!" she said, while her

class gathered up their mats and prepared to depart. "I never know what you will get up to next. Are you serious about this kazoo band?"

"Yep. We are going to play for the rest homes and anywhere else we can find a captive audience. We'll give folks a laugh and my people will get to perform. You know as well as I do, how invisible old people sometimes feel. Besides, it's good exercise. Marching around blowing into a kazoo is as good as a visit to the gym and lots more fun. Some of these Wrinkly Keesters have breathing problems, so this will be good therapy for them, too."

Tillie walked over to the CD player, switched off the serene sounds of flute music and rippling water, and slipped the CD into her capacious tote bag.

Slim rolled up her mat and handed it to her.

"I'd better round up my musicians and take them back to our practice room. Shall we get together later for a bite?" he asked.

"I'm having an old friend over for lunch today, but you can come for dinner, if you want. Only we'll have to eat early. I've got my Braille class this evening."

"Braille? Are you losing your sight? Why didn't you tell me?" Slim asked, obviously concerned.

"Silly!" Tillie responded with a smile. "I'm simply learning Braille to keep my brain flexible. It's one type of language I'd never studied. It's fascinating, and who knows when it might come in handy?"

"Sure, like Dumi, or Salishan, or one of those other exotic languages nobody speaks, anymore, except you," Slim said.

"You never know," she said. "Besides, learning new languages is wonderful mental exercise. You'll see. When you are hopelessly gaga, I'll still have my wits about me, thanks to learning all these languages."

"You can have 'em. What good will it be to

have your wits, if you can only communicate in gibberish?" Slim asked.

"I won't lose my native tongue, simply because I learn new ones..." she began, before seeing the twinkle in Slim's eye. "Oh you! Go on. I'll see you tonight. It's pork chops and rice."

"Yum! I'll bring my appetite," Slim said and began rounding up his kazoo players for the march back to their meeting room in another part of the senior center.

Tillie smiled to herself and continued gathering up her things.

Slim was a good friend. She was blessed and she knew it. Almost half-way through her eighty-fifth year and she still had her health, an active social life, and good friends. Not many folks could say the same.

Of course, she hadn't lived all these years without a measure of grief. Her beloved husband, Gerald, a renowned archaeologist, had developed Alzheimer's in his early sixties and died before reaching retirement age. Standing by him during his heartbreaking decline had spurred Tillie to a regimen of cerebral calisthenics, as she called them, to keep growing new brain cells and, hopefully, avoid a similar sad fate.

Regular physical and mental exercise was simply good stewardship. Her motto was *mens sana in corpore sano;* a healthy mind in a healthy body.

Decades earlier, Tillie's first experience of tragedy and pain had arrived when her only child, Gordon, was a teenager. Shortly after his fifteenth birthday, he'd made the winning touchdown for his high school team, and then collapsed and died in the end-zone from a previously undiagnosed heart defect.

Sudden catastrophe can either destroy a couple or bring them closer together. It was the latter for Tillie and Gerald. They had clung together in their pain, strengthening a love which, for Tillie, still endured.

"Tillie, excuse me," a small, bird-like woman, a new member of the class, tugged at Tillie's flowing sleeve.

"Yes?"

"Um, I was wondering, well, I don't mean to intrude, but we were talking and one of the ladies in the class was telling me you might be able to give me some advice, if you aren't too busy, that is," Olivette Vernon said.

"Advice about what? I'm happy to help, if I can," Tillie said, leaning one hip against a table and giving Olivette her full attention.

"It's my husband, Kendall. He's a dear man, but, um…as you may know, we moved here only last month from Bannoch, just down the coast. Kendall pastored the Reformed Church there for almost forty years. Such a stirring preacher! We moved to the assisted-living facility here because, well, you know, he didn't want to retire, you see, only his health… Oh, dear, I'm telling this all muddled. The sad fact is, he has Alzheimer's. I hope you aren't offended, but I heard about your husband. I didn't mean to pry into your personal life, of course, but…well, I hoped we might get together for a chat sometime, because, well, I thought you might know what it's like," she spoke rapidly, looking down at her hands.

"Of course," Tillie said, smiling. "I do know what it was like, at least for me. I can't know exactly what you are going through, but I'm happy to provide a listening ear. Why don't we go have a cup of coffee, right now?"

"Could we? You don't mind? Don't you have someplace to be?" Olivette twittered, teary-eyed.

"No place more important. Come along," Tillie said, putting her arm around the thin woman as they walked to the exit.

*

In the coffee shop, next to the senior center, Tillie led Olivette to a booth in the front window and nodded to the waitress.

"What can I get you, Mrs. T.? We've got a fresh batch of those cranberry-nut muffins you like," the waitress said with a smile.

"Sounds delectable, Amanda! I'll have one, with a cup of hot tea. What would you like, Olivette?"

"Just coffee, thanks," Olivette replied.

"Bring my friend a muffin, too," Tillie told the waitress. "She needs to add a bit of cushioning."

"I don't usually eat anything between meals," Olivette protested.

"How old are you? If you don't mind my asking," Tillie said.

"I'm sixty-eight. Why?"

"An older woman needs a little bit of lovely cushioning to stay healthy and as insurance against fragile bones, that's why. A mature woman should be like a ripe peach; soft and sweet; that's my motto," Tillie said, patting her own well-padded stomach. "Besides, our brains need a steady supply of nourishment to keep working. Strict diets kill

21

brain cells."

The waitress slid their steaming muffins and drinks onto the table, along with packets of butter, cream cheese, and a variety of jellies and jams.

"Those muffins do smell good," Olivette exclaimed. "I believe I'll try a small taste, after all."

Tillie tore a good-sized chunk from her warm muffin, slathered it with butter and marmalade, and popped it into her mouth before pouring milk into a hot cup of strong, black tea.

After nibbling on a tiny bite of muffin, Olivette followed Tillie's example and added cream cheese and a dollop of strawberry jam to a larger piece.

"That was tasty," she admitted, looking with surprise at her now empty plate.

"It's no sin to enjoy your food, you know, Olivette," Tillie said with a wry grin.

"I was raised rather strictly, I'm afraid. My father was a minister who leaned toward self-denial. My sister and I were raised on *A Pilgrim's*

Progress, instead of Mother Goose."

"From what I've read about the author of *A Pilgrim's Progress*, John Bunyan enjoyed his food when he could get it. What about his descriptions of the food served for supper in the Palace Beautiful?" Tillie asked.

"The 'meat, and fat things' you mean?" Olivette laughed. "I suppose being in prison while he was writing may have whetted his appetite."

"How are you adjusting to life in Tillamook?" Tillie asked, giving her new friend an opening to talk about her situation.

"Our apartment in Golden Memories assisted-living center is quite nice. It's rather small, but so much more modern and airy than our parsonage in Bannoch. I love the way the sunshine pours in on fine days."

"And is your husband adjusting to his retirement?"

Olivette looked down at her hands which were twisting her napkin. When she raised her head, Tillie saw tears in her new friend's eyes.

"He's not doing very well, at all," Olivette finally whispered.

"You said he has Alzheimer's," Tillie prompted. "Is it progressing?"

Olivette nodded, sniffing.

"When it first began," she said. "It was just little things; forgetting where he'd parked the car or put his keys. Then he began to lose his place in his sermon notes. He'd been working very hard, so I thought he just needed a rest. We spent a couple of days with my sister in Portland, visiting the museums and rose gardens. When we returned, he seemed better, but a few Sundays later he stopped in the middle of his sermon and walked down the church aisle and out the door. He'd forgotten where he was and panicked. Not forgotten where he was in the message, you understand, but where he was, physically. After that, I took him to the doctor and he was diagnosed. The rest, as they say, is history."

"So, how is he now? Does he still recognize

you?" Tillie asked.

"Sometimes," Olivette said.

"Oh, dear, I'm so sorry!" Tillie said. "I remember the first time Gerald thought I was a stranger. He refused to believe I was his wife. He said his wife was young and pretty, not a fat, old woman. He got so upset, I had to leave the room while the attendant calmed him down. When I think of it, even now, I still remember the pain."

"Yes. That is the worst part, isn't it?" Olivette agreed. "We want to stand by in sickness and health; to go through everything together. Being rejected, or worse yet, feared, is unbearable."

"But, you said Kendall still has lucid moments?"

"Fewer every day, but I cherish those times. My sister tried to convince me to put him into a home and get on with my own life. She doesn't understand; I don't want to miss a single one of those precious lucid moments when I have my dear Kendall back, again."

"I understand," Tillie said.

"Thank you. There is a support group at the housing complex, but I haven't felt comfortable sharing, yet."

"Have you had a chance to check out the local attractions?" Tillie asked. "You've probably toured the cheese factory, but have you been to the Quilt Museum?"

"I haven't been to the museum, no, but we often drove up to the cheese factory when we lived in Bannoch. Kendall is especially fond of squeaky cheese."

"Oh, yes! We are all fans of those cheese curds," Tillie said. "Say, why don't we plan a day to tour the Quilt Museum together? Some of the antique quilts are amazing."

"I'd like that," Olivette said.

"And whenever you need a listening ear, I am happy to get together with you, Olivette. I'll give you my number," Tillie said, digging around in her bright yellow bag for her business cards.

"That's a lovely purse," Olivette said. "It matches your tights and the swirls in your colorful blouse."

"Bright colors make me happy and yellow is my favorite. For years I avoided wearing it because it didn't flatter my complexion. Wasn't that silly?

"As a school teacher," she continued. "I thought I should wear conservative clothes. Then, after Gerald died, I spent a few months in the drab colors appropriate to my widowhood. One day I couldn't face another miserable, depressing outfit. I pulled everything out of my closet and piled all the drab clothes on the floor. When the only thing left hanging was a colorful caftan from one of Gerald's expeditions to the Middle East, I headed to the mall and bought clothes that made me feel good, either for their comfort or color. I didn't pay a bit of attention to whether anything was practical or age-appropriate, either. When I got home, I bagged up my old wardrobe and gave it away. I've never regretted it."

"How brave," Olivette said.

"Forget being appropriate and dress for joy; that's my motto. Do you always wear neutrals, like now?"

"Oh, yes. A pastor's wife doesn't want to be seen as too fashion-conscious. I've always tried to blend into the background as much as possible."

"You aren't a pastor's wife, anymore, though. What is your favorite color?"

"Deep purple," Olivette confessed. "Since I was a small child, I've been drawn to shades of purple. Isn't that awful? I suppose I have a subconscious desire to be treated like royalty."

"Tsk! We need to do something about this," Tillie said. "I have a lunch date I can't reschedule, so we won't be able to do it today, but next week I am going to take you shopping, right after class. No, don't object," she said when Olivette began to demur. "It will be my pleasure. I'm blessed with a comfortable income and I won't miss a few dollars to give you a much-needed treat."

Tillie handed Olivette her business card and rose from the table.

Before slipping it into her handbag, Olivette looked at the card. "Tillamook Tillie's Ripe and Ready Yoga" was printed in bright colors on one side and on the other were her address, phone number, and email.

Tillie paid their check and the two ladies went out. After a quick hug, Olivette hurried to the parking lot where she'd left her car and Tillie walked over to the bus stop.

The weather had been unsettled all morning, but the clouds seemed to be breaking up when the bus pulled in.

Quickly finding a seat on the half-empty bus, Tillie began to think about lunch preparations as the bus carried her down the familiar street.

She'd set a batch of whole-grain rolls to rise before yoga class and planned to pop them into the oven to serve warm with the meal. She mentally reviewed the contents of her pantry to plan the accompanying dishes.

The bus driver slammed on the brakes, jerking them to a stop. Tillie looked up and noticed they were in front of the high school.

A student on a motorbike had zipped into the parking lot, crossing in front of the bus, and forced the driver to stop.

Tillie looked at her watch and saw the student was late for class. The incident pulled her thoughts back to her many years of teaching school and she passed the rest of the bus ride in a pleasant meander down Memory Lane.

3

"**Hey**, Shantee! Wait up!" Samantha called as she hurried down the crowded school corridor toward her first period class.

"Hi Sam," Shantee said, edging closer to a bank of lockers to avoid the flow of noisy students while she waited for her friend.

"Have you seen Honora this morning?" Samantha said. "She was supposed to call me last night to share her notes from Chem class, but she never called. I need them to review before the quiz,"

"I haven't seen her. Maybe she's already in class."

The two girls entered their homeroom, but Honora wasn't there.

When their teacher called roll, she still hadn't arrived.

"Honora's never been late before," Samantha whispered, leaning forward over her desk toward Shantee.

Shantee turned her head to reply, but the teacher clapped her hands and called the class to order.

*

Across town, inside a neat-looking bungalow in a pleasant tree-lined neighborhood, Mr. and Mrs. Anniston were becoming more agitated by the moment.

Honora's mother, Ruth, a slight matron with faded red-hair, perched on the edge of a beige and cream striped wing chair, looking anxiously at her husband as he clicked off his phone.

"Well, what did they say?" she asked.

"It's still too soon. She has to be missing twenty-four hours. The officer tried to assure me that she'll soon turn up. I got the feeling he thinks our daughter ran away."

"Not Honora! Howard, you know she

32

would never do anything like that," Ruth protested.

Mr. Anniston, a tall middle-aged man dressed for the office in slacks, a white shirt, and a blue-striped tie, ran his hand through his thinning dark blond hair, leaving a few tufts jutting out at odd angles.

"I know that, and you know that, but the police don't know her like we do. They assume she's some typical, flighty teenager. The officer did promise to spread the word to the patrol units to keep an eye out for her, and he said if she hasn't returned by dinnertime tonight, they will open a missing persons case."

"By dinnertime? After she could have been lying in a ditch, badly injured, all night long? We can't just sit here!"

Ruth jumped up and began to pace.

"We've called the school and all her friends. What more can we do?" Howard asked.

"We can go looking for her. Come on!" she

said, grabbing a jacket from the coat tree in the hall on her way out.

Still putting his arms into the sleeves of his raincoat, Mr. Anniston joined his wife on the sidewalk.

Although it was not raining at the moment, the large dark clouds filling the late March sky were growing closer together and threatening to burst open.

"Where do we start?" he asked.

Mrs. Anniston looked bewildered, wringing her hands and stepping out first in one direction and then the other.

"I guess we could retrace her route from the dance studio," her husband suggested.

"Yes! Of course! I'm so glad you stayed home from work this morning, Howard. My brain has stopped functioning."

He took his wife's trembling hand and the distraught couple started walking toward the park.

*

"Wait here, girls. Principal Wilson will see you in just a minute," Gladys, the school secretary said, gesturing for Samantha and Shantee to take a seat and returning to her desk behind the counter.

"What do you think the principal wants?" Samantha asked Shantee in a whisper.

"Beats me! I haven't done anything wrong. Have you?"

Gladys stood and leaned over the counter, saying, "Girls, you may go in, now."

When they entered her office, Mrs. Wilson nodded at the visitors' chairs, and the nervous girls sat.

"You two are good friends of Honora Anniston, I believe," Mrs. Wilson said and both girls nodded, exchanging a worried glance.

"Has something happened to Honora?" Samantha blurted.

"No, no, there is nothing to indicate anything untoward has happened. However, she

35

didn't return home last night and her parents are a little worried. They expected her to come straight home after dance class. Do either of you have any idea where she might have gone?"

"Gee, when we left class last night, Honora said she was heading home," Sam said.

"We offered to give her a ride in my brother's car, but she wanted to ride her bike," Shantee added.

After assuring the principal neither of them had any helpful information, the two girls, hall passes clutched in their hands, walked quietly back to class, each mentally turning over the previous day's events, trying to think of any clue that Honora might have been thinking of running off.

4

Tillie strolled between the raised beds in the herb garden behind her cottage, gathering basil and oregano for the pasta dish she was serving her friend, Opal Pyle, for lunch.

The rain which had threatened all morning had resulted in only a brief sprinkle before the wind swept the clouds toward the mountains, making way for welcome sunshine.

As she snipped damp leaves into her basket, Tillie spoke to Edgar, her red-footed tortoise, who was placidly enjoying the sun's warmth in his outdoor pen.

"You would have laughed, too, Edgar, if you had seen Slim's silly band. That man is a never-ending source of amazement and entertainment."

Edgar, well-acquainted with Slim's antics, and taciturn by nature, merely blinked.

37

Tillie sniffed the air and turned toward the house.

"My rolls!" she cried, scurrying inside and snatching a pan from the oven with a sigh of relief.

"Perfect," she said, piling the steaming hot golden rolls in a napkin-lined serving basket and covering them with an embroidered tea towel.

Tillie glanced at the pot of water simmering on the stove awaiting the pasta, and then lifted the lid on her sauce to toss in a handful of fresh herbs.

Satisfied with her lunch preparations, she went into her bedroom and changed into the same colorful caftan she'd mentioned to Olivette that morning. Pausing at the mirror to admire its age-mellowed paisley design, she tucked a stray lock of white hair behind one ear just as the doorbell rang.

Tillie's cat, Agatha, a silver-gray American Short-hair, followed her into the entry, then scooted off to the parlor when Tillie opened the door for her guest.

"Hi, Opal. Come on in," Tillie said, stepping

back to welcome her friend inside.

Almost a foot taller than Tillie and more than a decade younger, wearing faded jeans and a plaid flannel shirt, Opal Pyle stepped into the foyer and hugged her hostess.

She stepped back and handed over a jar of amber colored honey.

"Perfect! Liquid gold from your hives," Tillie exclaimed, holding it up to the light. "I love your thistle honey, Opal. Thank you! We can have some on our rolls."

"The bees are doing a bang-up job this year. I think they may finally be recovering from the nasty bee blight we've been dealing with the past few years," Opal replied, following Tillie through to the kitchen.

"I thought we'd eat on the veranda, since it's turned into such a nice day," Tillie said, handing her guest a tray filled with cutlery. "Fresh food should be eaten in the fresh air; that's my motto. I'm always thankful my porch catches the sun and blocks the wind so perfectly.

"Take those out and set the table while I just pop the pasta into the pot."

A few moments later, seated in well-padded wicker chairs with bowls of pasta, salmon salad, and fruit laid out on the blue and white checkered table cloth, the two friends chatted and waved to passersby as they enjoyed their meal.

They presented a charming tableau on the wide veranda. Framed by hanging baskets of red and white geraniums and blue petunias, interspersed with rustic wind chimes, they overlooked Tillie's front yard, which was dominated by a charming cottage garden enlivened with the comically grotesque gnome statuary she loved.

Drizzling thistle honey onto a buttered roll, Tillie wiped the dripping spoon with a fingertip and sucked her sticky digit clean before taking a bite of the roll.

"I'm glad you like my honey, Tillie," Opal

said. "My pantry is getting crowded."

"I can't believe you have any trouble giving away your surplus," Tillie remarked, dabbing at her mouth with a cloth napkin.

"I usually give a few quarts to Laura Breem. But, when I called her today to see when I could bring them by, she was too upset to even think about it. I never got around to asking her."

"What was bothering her?" Tillie asked, taking a sip of tea.

"Laura's great-niece has gone missing and Laura is beside herself."

"How old is her niece? Do I know her?"

"Honora is about sixteen, I think. She's the one I told you about... the dancer, remember?" Opal asked.

"Of course, I remember. I've got an excellent memory, you know," Tillie said. "Could she have just run off? Teenagers sometimes do that."

"Not Honora. She's not that sort of girl. She went to her dance class after school yesterday, just like always, and never came home. Her parents called the police last night and again this morning, but the officer they spoke with said she'd probably turn up. Laura's nephew, Howard, Honora's father, was really angry when they didn't send out a search party right away."

"I don't blame him. When did you speak to Laura? Maybe Honora has come home by now," Tillie suggested.

"I called just before coming over. Maybe I should call her again," Opal said, pulling out her cell phone.

Tillie cleared away the lunch things, giving her friend privacy for her phone call.

When she came back out to the porch, Opal's expression told her the girl was still missing.

"No news?" Tillie asked.

"I'm afraid not. You know, I think maybe I should go over to Laura's. She sounded so upset. Waiting alone has to be hard on her."

"Of course. You go ahead," Tillie said,

giving her friend a hug before Opal gathered up her things and left.

As soon as Tillie was alone, Agatha slipped out onto the porch and jumped onto a vacant chair, sniffing at the enticing salmon fragrance lingering in the air.

"The loss of a child is a terrible thing, Aggie," Tillie said to the cat.

She gathered the remaining lunch things onto a tray, and then paused to murmur a brief prayer for the missing girl and her family before taking the laden tray into the house.

*

The Annistons walked slowly along the bike path, peering into the shrubs and weeds flourishing beside the trail for any sign of their daughter, calling her name as they walked.

When they reached the far end of the path, they stopped, looking lost and confused.

"What now?" Howard asked. "Where else could she have gone?"

"Let's go all the way to the dance studio. It's just up the road. Maybe she had an accident before she even got to the park," Ruth suggested.

They were frantic for some sign of their daughter, but dreaded what they might find, as well.

It was both a disappointment and a relief when they failed to see any sign of an accident before reaching the dance studio.

The studio door was locked and a package leaning beside the entrance seemed to indicate no one had arrived, yet, that day.

They decided to retrace their steps through the park, still hoping to find some overlooked trace of their precious daughter.

5

An older model eighteen-wheeler sped south along the Coast Highway and took the turn-off toward Grants Pass, Oregon, to connect with the Interstate freeway. After traveling east a few miles, it pulled into a roadside truck stop and parked on the edge of the lot.

A swarthy middle-aged man with a thatch of oily black hair and the advancing paunch of a long-haul trucker climbed down from the cab. The rolled up sleeves on his stained shirt revealed heavily tattooed upper arms.

He hurried across the parking area carrying a full trash bag that he stuffed down into the gas station's dumpster, and then walked back to his rig, wiping his hands on a rag.

Grunting, he climbed back up into the cab and maneuvered the semi back onto the road, eager to make up time. His earlier detours had put him behind schedule.

It hadn't been on his itinerary, but when he saw the sweet-faced girl shivering in the rain beside the freeway on-ramp outside Portland, he couldn't resist a quick change of plans.

Replaying it all in his mind, now, gave him a rush.

Remembering how grateful she'd been when he stopped, he emitted an ugly bark of laughter. It was only when he'd turned off the highway onto a deserted country lane that she'd stopped chattering happily about her big adventure and fear finally shut her up. He'd drunk in the stark terror filling her eyes and knew his impulsive decision would be worth it.

As usual, it was all over too quickly, but that meant he'd been able to keep his appointment in Tillamook.

The trucker's dead black eyes glinted as he relived the hours just past. He smiled as he drove, revealing stained and broken teeth. With one hand he fingered a woman's bracelet hanging from a knob on the dash, savoring his memories and already feeling the uncontrollable hunger building, once more.

His own particular passion was as addictive as a drug, and like drugs, he needed constantly greater gratification, ever more frequently.

He scanned the highway ahead, always on the lookout for his next fix. Luckily for him, opportunities appeared around almost every bend in the road.

*

"Ooh," Honora moaned.

Her head hurt and she felt sick to her stomach. She tried to sit up in the total darkness, but her limbs wouldn't respond.

Gradually becoming more alert, but still unable to see, she blinked rapidly and felt her eyelashes brush against some sort of cloth covering the top part of her face. A blindfold?

Jerking her hands to try to remove the covering, she realized that her arms extending behind her head were being held there by something tied around her wrists. Slowly, her senses told her she was lying spread-eagled on her back on what felt like a narrow air mattress, and her ankles were held in place with rough cords or ropes.

The air smelled musty, of earth and rotten leaves.

Where was she? How did she get here?

She twisted and bucked in an attempt to get free, causing fresh pain and waves of nausea, but she couldn't get loose.

Terrified, she began to panic. What was going on?

"Is anyone there?" she croaked around the wad of cloth in her mouth. She tried to push it out with her tongue, but it wouldn't budge.

She didn't know where she was or how she'd gotten here, but she knew she was in a bad spot and totally helpless.

The grim reality of her situation hit her and she fought against hysteria by taking several deep breaths.

Her last memory was of leaving the dance class on her bike and heading home. After that, nothing.

Horrific images from movies and the news forced themselves into her mind. She fought against the bile rising in her throat and tried to scream, but only produced a gagging sound..

Although she was still wearing her jacket and a rough blanket covered her, she shivered with cold, as well as fear.

A faint rumbling noise broke through her rising panic. It grew louder, seeming to come from every direction at once, and dread squeezed her chest, stealing her breath. She gasped, her heart pounding in her ears. The sound grew more intense, and then faded away; only to be repeated and to eventually settle into a constant drone.

Again, she tried to scream for help, but the gag in her mouth still muffled the sound. Whimpering, with tears dampening her blindfold, she began to pray, desperately begging God for rescue.

*

A young policeman was seated at the Annistons' dining room table jotting in his notepad. Although it was the dinner hour, there were no cooking aromas competing with the pervasive atmosphere of despair.

"So, you haven't heard anything from your daughter since she left for school yesterday morning, is that right?" he asked.

Ruth sat across the table, biting her lips and trying not to cry in front of the policeman. She nodded.

Howard paced around the room, stopping only to reply to the officer's questions.

"That's right. We know she went to her dance class after school, though, as I said."

"Do you have a recent photo I can take with me?" the officer asked, standing. "And your daughter's toothbrush?" he added, not making eye contact.

"Why do you want her toothbrush?" Ruth asked, before turning pale as realization hit.

The toothbrush would have Honora's DNA on it.

"What are you going to do to find my daughter? We want her back alive, you know." Howard said, after Ruth stumbled out of the room.

"Of course, Mr. Anniston. I assure you we will do everything in our power to find your daughter and bring her home, safe and sound. She's probably fine, you know. These cases usually end when the missing girl has a spat with her boyfriend and comes running back home."

"Honora doesn't have a boyfriend, officer. She's kept busy with schoolwork and her dancing," Howard said. "She didn't go off voluntarily, I assure you. Someone has taken her, or she's had an accident and needs help."

Ruth, her eyes puffy and red, returned with a photo and the toothbrush in a small plastic bag. She handed them over before leaning into her husband's embrace with a sob.

"Thanks. We'll be in touch," the policeman said and escaped, leaving the distraught parents to try to comfort one another.

6

Outside a rustic cabin tucked amongst the evergreen trees near the California mountain community of Weed, the gentle murmuring of the wind in the trees was drowned out by the raised, angry voices of ex-Marine, Hope Masterson, and her boyfriend, Chad.

A gunshot rang out and was followed by sounds of a struggle and a body being slammed to the floor.

After a few moments of silence, Hope, a tall, muscular, redhead, wearing a combat jacket over jeans and a sweatshirt, stormed out, letting the rusty screen door slam behind her.

She stomped across the plank porch, hefting her duffel bag over one shoulder, and hopped down into the bare dirt yard, angrily kicking pine cones out of her path.

Chad, dressed in boxer shorts and a torn tee shirt, staggered into the doorway, shouting curses at her retreating form.

"Hope! Come on back! Don't leave like this," he yelled when she ignored him. "Let's talk this out!"

Hope turned to face him.

"There's nothing to talk about. Nobody pulls a gun on me and gets a second chance. Nobody," she said.

Chad stepped across the porch and sunlight revealed a large bruise on his shoulder, a swollen eye, and several cuts and scrapes still oozing blood.

"Come on, it was an accident! I didn't think it was even loaded," he called.

"Forget it!" Hope yelled over her shoulder and continued walking toward the road.

Chad jumped off the porch, as if to follow her in his bare feet, but stepped on a sharp pine cone, yelped in pain, and limped back to his cabin, swearing and shaking his head.

Marching down the dirt logging road, Hope's anger and adrenaline melted away. She felt lighter with every step.

This blowup had been brewing for a long time and she was glad it was finally over. She knew Chad was unstable from all the drugs he took, but she never expected him to try to shoot her.

Luckily, her military training had kicked in and saved her skin. Keeping up with her physical training after leaving the Marines had been a good move.

Dealing with Chad's moods and demands was behind her, now, and she was ready to shake the dust off and start fresh.

When Hope reached the end of the logging road and set her boots on the asphalt of the winding mountain highway, she mentally tossed a coin and turned her face to the north. She hadn't been to the ocean in ages and she was ready to let the sea breezes blow the past few months away.

*

Slim Bottoms parked his elderly Cadillac sedan in the garage and walked out to check his mailbox before going into his house.

"More trash for recycling, as usual," he said, sorting through the bundle of advertisements and appeals for donations.

He smiled when he saw an envelope with a handwritten address.

"Well, now, this is a treat," he said.

Entering his home through the back door, he dropped the junk mail into the recycling bin and carried his envelope through to the kitchen where he set it on the table beside a single place mat.

He made a cup of instant coffee and sat at the table to enjoy reading the letter from his grandson, Sylvester.

"Hi Gramps," it began, as usual. "Everything's good here with Eula and the kids. How are things with you?"

Slim sipped his coffee while reading the letter, smiling, shaking his head, and occasionally chuckling.

Sylvester and his family had lived in England, in one of the suburbs of London, since Sylvester's company transferred him in the nineties. They adjusted quickly and now considered themselves Brits.

Slim made the trip to visit the family every couple of years and enjoyed infrequent video chats on the computer with his great-grandchildren, a boy and a girl. He couldn't get over the kids' British accents every time he heard them.

He wished he could see them more often and wondered how much longer he would be up to enduring the long intercontinental flights. However, it was pretty pricey for the whole family to come to him, so he would make the effort as long as he could.

The first time he'd flown "across the pond" had been with his late wife, Joyce, the year after Sylvester relocated. Slim remembered how frightened she'd been, clinging to his hand for the entire thirteen-hour flight. Their only son, Mark, Sylvester's father, had died of a heart attack only a year before the trip. Joyce was determined to stay in touch with their remaining family.

His wife had been a shy little thing for most of their marriage, but she had found the strength and courage of a tiger during the years of her losing struggle against breast cancer. It was almost ten years since she died, but he still missed her.

Slim slipped the letter back into its envelope and carried it into his study.

This room had been his home office, as well as his retreat, during his long and successful career as an architect.

He still used the drafting table to design everything from home improvement projects to fantastic, futuristic buildings. Although he seldom brought these plans to fruition, he enjoyed the process.

Tillie had her methods of staving off dementia and Slim had his.

Sitting at his desk, he moved a recent copy of Architectural Digest and pulled out a pad and pen from his desk drawer to compose a response to Sylvester's letter. He planned to tell him all about the Wrinkly Keesters and Tillie's comical reaction.

In truth, many of the silly things Slim did were just so he could have something entertaining to share in his correspondence with his grandson.

They sent emails, now and then, but Slim and Sylvester shared a common love of old-fashioned letters. There was something so tactile and intimate about writing and receiving physical letters which made it worth the extra time and effort.

Pausing to think, Slim leaned back in his vintage Eames chair and looked through the wide window, out beyond the pine trees to the sliver of Tillamook Bay beyond. He'd designed this house with the views in mind and never tired of the scenery before him.

The house was too big for a single man, of

course, but he would never leave it. A few times a year he hired a cleaning service to come in to wash windows and shovel out the dust bunnies, so his poor housekeeping wouldn't leave him living in squalor.

The year before, he'd gotten up the gumption to ask Tillie to marry him and come share his home, but she turned him down.

He'd been disappointed, but he understood.

It was hard to make changes at their age. Besides, she couldn't face being disloyal to Gerald. Still loved him, of course.

Well, Slim loved Joyce, too, but that didn't keep him from having feelings for Tillie.

He picked up his pen to finish the letter to Sylvester. He wasn't about to tell the boy about his romantic life, so he wrote in his elegant old-fashioned cursive about a recent senior citizens bus tour. Taking only a few minor liberties with the truth, he managed to make a rather mundane event sound comical in the extreme.

When he finished the letter, he was hungry, so he rummaged in the refrigerator, pulling out an assortment of leftovers Tillie had sent home with him from their last meal at her place.

He popped a plate of chicken stew with dumplings into the microwave and poured himself a beer while it heated, then took his lunch into the living room and turned on the TV.

7

A small television on the kitchen counter was broadcasting the local evening news, and Tillie was fluffing steamed rice with a fork, when Slim arrived later that afternoon.

"It's open!" she called out in response to his knock.

Walking through the hall, Slim stopped to admire a framed picture hanging on the wall.

"Is this watercolor painting of the trees new?" he called.

"Yes, I just got it back from the framer. I was trying a *plein aire* technique in that stretch of park bordering the slough. I thought I'd get eaten alive by mosquitoes before finishing it."

"It's nice," he said.

"I think it turned out well, too. Thanks. I just heard they are searching that very park for the poor girl who's gone missing. They'll have a big job covering those acres of undisturbed wilderness. I feel for her, if she's lying hurt out there."

"Something smells good," Slim said, stepping into the kitchen, lifting the lid on a pan of pork chop gravy, and giving it a stir.

"You can get the plates down, if you want to make yourself useful," Tillie said.

They took their plates, filled with browned chops and steaming gravy-covered rice, into the dining room, where the side dishes and place settings awaited them.

Slim said a brief prayer of thanks before reaching for the basket of dinner rolls.

"You just make these?" he asked.

"I set them to rise before yoga and baked them when my friend, Opal, came to lunch. She didn't have much appetite, so these were left over," Tillie said.

"No appetite for your good food? Was she sick?"

Tillie was explaining Opal's connection to the missing teenager when she paused, listening. The television was still on in the kitchen and something the announcer said caught her attention.

"Excuse me," she said, getting up. "I want to hear this."

Slim followed her into the kitchen to see the news story about a young girl's body being found in Oceanside, just up the coast.

"Oh, dear! I hope that isn't Opal's friend's great-niece," Tillie said.

"The reporter said they haven't made an identification, so let's not borrow trouble," Slim said, patting Tillie's shoulder.

"Yes. Sufficient unto the day are the troubles therein…that's my motto," she said, snapping off the TV. "We'd better eat or I'll be late for my class."

*

Honora had cried herself to sleep and when she woke again, she was devastated as soon as she realized her situation was real and not the nightmare she'd hoped.

"Hello?" she tried to call out, but hearing her gagged and garbled voice filled her with anguish and a renewed sense of her helplessness.

Where was she? What should she do? How was she going to get free?

Fighting rising hysteria, she clung to her birthday memory verse; *Have I not commanded you? Be strong and courageous. Do not be afraid; do not be discouraged, for the LORD your God will be with you wherever you go.*

The Bible verse from the first chapter of the book of Joshua was what she needed to cling to, now. Even in this place, God was with her.

Ever since she was tiny, Honora's parents had given her a special Bible verse for each of her birthdays. She read and repeated the verse every morning and at bedtime each night throughout the year. She'd never imagined how much she would need this verse when she'd received it on her last birthday.

Taking several deep breaths, she tried to recall all of her birthday verses, seeing how far back she could go, and grunting them around her gag into the blackness.

When her heart began to race from her terror creeping back in, she went back to the verse in Joshua and started over.

*

"Here we are, Tillie girl," Slim said, pulling up at the high school entrance. "Call me when you're done and I'll swoop in on my chariot to carry you off home."

"Thanks," Tillie said with a smile as she stepped out.

Slim drove off with a wave and a toot of the horn as Tillie climbed the broad concrete steps to the school entrance.

She consciously swept her mind clear of thoughts of the missing girl and prepared to concentrate on learning Braille. The language was more difficult than she'd expected. She grasped the concepts quickly enough, but recognizing the patterns of raised bumps was proving to be elusive.

In the classroom, she slipped into her seat just as the lesson began.

After class, the half-dozen students lingered around a small refreshments table, chatting and nibbling on the prepackaged cookies their teacher provided.

Gathering up her things, Tillie caught snatches of several conversations, all centered on the missing Anniston girl.

"I heard she ran off to New York to join the Rockettes," one ill-informed woman said.

"My Fred is joining the local search party, bright and early tomorrow morning!" someone else boasted.

"They won't find anything, I'll bet. Probably that serial killer we've been hearing about the past couple of years got her."

"Didn't they already find her body up around Oceanside?" asked another.

"The description fits, according to what they said on my car radio while I was driving to class," someone replied.

Tillie decided to give the rumor-infused refreshments a pass. She was seldom tempted by store bought cookies and gossip always left a sour taste in her mouth.

"Least said, soonest mended, that's my motto," she said under her breath.

As she hurried out into the empty corridor, Tillie collided with the cleaning lady's cart, knocking rolls of paper towels and a spray bottle to the floor.

"Pardon me!" Tillie said. "I was digging for my phone and not looking where I was going. I'm so sorry. Here, let me help you."

"Don't bother," the tired-looking middle-aged woman replied. "My boy'll get those things."

Turning to the gangly young man hanging back in the shadows, she said, "Danny, come over here and help me."

Her son shuffled forward and picked up the cleaning supplies, then immediately slipped around the corner.

"Your son's a little shy," Tillie said. "I'm a retired school teacher, so I recognize the signs. My name's Tillie Thistlethwaite."

"Marjie Whipple," the woman replied with a nod. "My Danny is a bit standoffish with strangers, but he's a good boy. He doesn't like me to go out to work nights all by myself, especially with all the horrible things happening around here, lately, like that young girl gettin' raped and murdered on her way home from dancing class."

"I'm sure. Well, it was nice meeting you," Tillie said, excusing herself and walking toward the exit to call Slim.

It seemed everyone was convinced the body found in Oceanside belonged to their missing girl. Couldn't anyone hold out a little hope for a happy ending?

"Hey, Mrs. T. Hold up!" a voice called out.

Turning, Tillie saw a classmate, Amy Grider, a former student from her teaching days. Now a gray-haired grandmother, Amy was learning Braille for a handicapped grandson.

"Can I give you a lift home, Mrs. T.?" Amy offered.

"I was just about to call my friend for a ride, but I'm happy to spare him the trip. Thank you, Amy," Tillie said. "I'll just text him, so he knows he can go to bed."

Tillie had conquered the art of sending text messages on her phone only a few months before and she was still feeling rather proud of herself for this up-to-date accomplishment.

While walking to Amy's car, they noticed the fog had rolled in to surround streetlights with misty halos.

Moisture dripped from eaves and tree limbs by the time Amy parked her car in front of Mrs. T's. bungalow. She kept the car idling at the curb while her former teacher trotted up the walk to her door.

Before stepping onto her porch, Tillie paused in the glow from an ornate brass light fixture, a souvenir from a long ago archaeological expedition, and detoured into her front garden.

Up to her knees in a riotous variety of early spring blooms, she carefully tucked up the vines on a rambling rose and stooped down to straighten one of her funny little gnomes, then bustled inside, fluttering a wave to Amy as she closed the door.

Amy chuckled to herself. Practical Mrs. T. was the last person she ever expected to dote on kitschy garden gnomes. Would pink flamingos be next?

8

At first light the next morning, the small Tillamook police force, along with a contingent of county sheriff's deputies and local volunteers, began looking for the missing girl, concentrating on the area between the dance studio and her home.

They gathered at the mid-city park at the tip of Tillamook Bay. The area was crisscrossed with wooded nature trails.

Retracing Honora's usual path through the park, they soon found the broken headlamp from her bicycle under some bushes near the pathway, although the bike didn't turn up.

In mid-morning, the leader of a Scout troop helping with the search called a policeman over to a stone retaining wall.

"I think I've found something, officer," he said, pointing to a massive red stain running down the wall.

The policeman, at first startled, approached the wall for a closer look and smiled.

"It's not blood, sir. See that tree?" he pointed to the other side of the wall. "It's a pomegranate tree. This is pomegranate juice. Looks like someone's used this wall to smash open the fruit."

The Scout Master saw remnants of last season's pomegranate peels and pith lying in the weeds at the base of the wall and blushed.

"Sorry, officer," he said.

"Not at all. You should alert us to anything suspicious. This could have been evidence of a crime. But, let's hope we'll find our girl alive and well," the officer reassured the man, patting his shoulder, and they both resumed the search.

*

The following morning, when Sheriff's Detective John Ransom arrived at the Oregon State Police station in Tillamook to oversee the joint case, he was met by an excited officer with a scruffy man in tow.

"Sir! This guy was camping in the park, under the bridge. He had the missing girl's backpack on him," the policeman said, holding out the bag to Ransom.

"Good work, Willis," Ransom said. "Put him in an interview room and stay with him. I'll take the backpack to Forensics and be right with you."

"Could this case be solved so easily?" Ransom wondered.

He hated missing kids cases and would like to have this one off his hands ASAP.

Slipping on disposable gloves, he rummaged through the bag. He removed the cell phone and, noting that it was password protected, returned it to the bag. Finding nothing else of immediate interest, he dropped it at the lab, tossing the used gloves in the trash on his way.

After reviewing the case files, he headed for the interview room, stopping on his way for a cup of the infamous station house coffee. He tasted the hot, inky liquid, made a face, and added several spoons of sugar before walking to the interview cubicle.

Entering the sparsely furnished room, Ransom nodded to the deputy, and sat down at the table across from the man cowering in the other chair.

After taking a sip of bitter coffee, he set the cup aside and opened the file, making a show of examining the few entries on the mostly blank forms. It was a tactic he often used to unsettle a suspect.

"Name?" he demanded, suddenly leaning forward.

The man, who had been slumped in his chair, jerked upright at the detective's abrupt question.

"Muh, my, my name is Orlie Jones," he cried.

Ransom checked the form, as though doubting the man's truthfulness.

"What were you doing with that backpack,

Mr. *Jones*?" Ransom asked.

"Nothin'. I just found it in the bushes. I didn't steal it, honest," Jones whined.

Ransom paused to take another drink from his mug and made a note in the file before asking his next question.

"Why didn't you turn the bag in? You didn't think it was yours, did you?"

"No, sir. I figured someone just threw it away."

"That bag was full of textbooks and personal belongings. Why would anyone throw it away? Couldn't you tell it belonged to a student? Don't tell me you haven't heard of the missing girl?"

Jones squirmed and peered intently at a corner of the room, as though hoping to find an answer there.

"Kids throw stuff away all the time. Coulda' been anyone," he mumbled, looking down.

"Did you see someone throw away the bag?"

"No, sir. Like I said, I just found it. It was back under a bush in some weeds and stuff. I didn't do nothin' wrong!"

"Was there anyone around when you found it?" Ransom asked.

Jones shook his head.

"Speak up, man!" Ransom snapped.

"Yessir! I mean, no sir, there wasn't nobody around."

"Officer Willis, take this man back to the park and have him show you exactly where the bag was found, then book him. He must have at least one or two outstanding warrants. We don't want him to wander off before we get this cleared up."

Ransom's gut instinct told him this drug-addled man had nothing to do with the missing girl, but he wasn't willing to cut him loose, just yet, in case he remembered something of value.

Back in his office, Ransom was interrupted by a deputy placing a report on his desk.

"They identified that body up by Oceanside.

She was a runaway from Portland," the deputy said. "Not our girl, after all."

"Thanks. Do they know how she died?"

"All indications are she's the latest victim of the Coastal Killer, you know, that trucker who's been dropping bodies all up and down the state the past couple of years. She was strangled, stabbed, and dumped, just like the others. "

"Did they find anything to help us identify that monster, this time?"

The deputy frowned and shook his head.

"This guy has been getting away with his grisly deeds for far too long. He's got to make a mistake, sooner or later," Ransom said.

"If he doesn't leave us any clues, there's not much we can do," the deputy said. "It's not like we can put up roadblocks on all the highways and stop and search every truck."

"We don't even have any proof it definitely is a trucker," Ransom said in disgust. "Whoever he is, I hope our local girl didn't run into him."

"My daughter, Clarissa, takes dancing lessons with the Anniston girl. She says Honora was really good, but her folks wouldn't let her go away to try out at any of the big city dance companies. Maybe she decided to run off on her own," the deputy suggested.

"That's an idea. We should have sent her description to all the buses, train stations, and airports. Has that been done?" Ransom asked. "Let's hope she'd have enough sense not to try hitchhiking."

"That's routine, but I'll go make sure it's been done, just in case. We don't get many of these kinds of cases."

"Thanks," Ransom said and picked up the phone to find out for himself if this angle was being covered to his satisfaction. As the deputy said, they weren't familiar with many of these cases, thankfully, and if the girl had run off to the bright lights of the big city, they needed to find her before she became the Coastal Killer's next victim

9

Pulling into an industrial area parking lot on the outskirts of Grants Pass, the trucker finished the last of his hamburgers and climbed down from his cab. He wandered along the weedy shoulder of the access road and relieved himself with a groan before walking up and down to stretch his legs. Climbing back into the cab, he crawled into the sleeper compartment and popped open a beer from his tiny refrigerator. Leaning back against the side of the cab, he allowed himself to relish the events of the day.

He'd left Portland early and was scarcely on his way when he'd picked up that sweet little hitchhiker. He'd dropped her near a turnout in Oceanside without hardly losing any time, then got to Tillamook by late afternoon, as he'd planned.

He liked to travel through Tillamook,

80

whenever he could. He had an aunt who lived there when he was a kid. He used to stay with her whenever his mother, a drug addicted prostitute, was in jail. His aunt wasn't much better, but at least she didn't beat him or let her boyfriends mess with him. His only happy childhood memories happened in Tillamook and he went back as often as possible.

Lots of good stuff happens in Tillamook.

*

Cramped and hungry in the darkness, Honora struggled to keep her wits about her and resist being overwhelmed by the shock of her situation.

Forcing herself to think about the night of her capture, she focused on every detail she could remember, searching for clues to the person who had taken her, and why.

Everything had seemed so ordinary, except that weird feeling of being watched after she'd ridden into the trees. She recalled her growing anxiety and how she'd dismissed it as an overactive imagination when she heard that twig snap, but she couldn't recall the moment she was attacked.

Honora blamed herself for not accepting a ride home with Shantee and Samantha. She hadn't wanted to mess with the hassle of getting her bike into James's trunk.

Stupid!

Going through the park after sunset was pretty stupid, too.

The least she could have done was keep her phone in her hand as she rode. Then maybe she could have called for help before she was grabbed. Of course, she'd stupidly kept her phone in her backpack when she cycled.

She wondered about her backpack. Maybe the guy brought it here, too, wherever "here" was. If she could get loose and find that backpack, and if her phone was still in it, she could call for help.

And if she were a butterfly she could fly over the rainbow, too.

Stupid!

With a moan of frustration, she twisted and turned against her ropes and tried again to spit out the nasty gag. The cloth wicked every drop of moisture from her mouth, leaving it feeling swollen and furry.

"Oh, God," she began to pray again. "Are you here with me as the Bible verse says?"

*

Standing at the dance studio entrance digging the keys out of her satchel, Mimsy Waits noticed a parcel at her feet. The label was hand-lettered, saying simply, *Dance Teacher*, so she picked it up and carried it inside.

She set the package down on her desk and began preparing for the day's lessons; lining up the music on the CD player and digging the practice props from the cupboard, then cleaning the smudges off the mirror wall.

She told the girls to keep their hands off the mirror, but after every session the shiny surface was dotted with fingerprints and, sometimes, even lip prints, or hearts with initials written in condensation from the girls' breath.

"What is it with teenage girls?" she wondered, spraying window cleaner.

When everything was in order, Mimsy remembered the parcel.

She rummaged for scissors in a desk drawer, cut the string, and tore off the packing tape. Opening the box, she discovered a beautiful carving of a ballet dancer nestled in a protective bed of crumpled tissue paper.

Mimsy stood the carving on her desk and rummaged through the paper, looking for a packing slip or a note, but there was nothing more.

Carrying the carving closer to the window for a better look, she was struck by how much it resembled her star dance student, Honora. Apparently the girl had an artistic secret admirer.

She wasn't too surprised, Honora was not only a talented dancer and a beautiful young woman, she was also a thoroughly sweet and gentle person.

Still, the dance teacher couldn't completely stifle a pang of envy. No one had ever wanted to make a sculpture or painting of Mimsy, not even when she was young and slim and dancing professionally.

Mimsy decided to show the mysterious gift to Honora when she arrived for her lesson after school, but when the other girls arrived for class Honora wasn't among them.

Mimsy asked her friends where she was.

"Didn't you hear?" Samantha said. "She's gone missing! She never went home last night."

"Yeah," Shantee said. "Her folks called mine last night and when she didn't show up at school today, the principal asked us if we knew where she was."

Mimsy worried about her favorite student all through the class. If she didn't return, the performance would be a bust, but Mimsy really liked the girl, as well. It wasn't a bit like Honora to go off and not tell anyone.

It seemed really odd, too, that someone dropped off a carving of her on the day after she went missing. Mimsy had a bad feeling in the pit of her stomach.

After class she phoned her neighbor, Laura Breem, the girl's great-aunt.

"Hello, Laura?" she said when Mrs. Breem answered. "This is Mimsy, from next door. I just heard about Honora. I'm so sorry! I don't mean to bother you, but an odd package was left here at the dance studio and I would like to come over and show it to you when I get home, if that's okay. Great. I'll see you in about fifteen minutes. Bye!"

10

Detective Ransom poured over case notes and progress reports all afternoon and was getting nowhere. Frustrated, he sighed, ran his fingers through his short brown hair, and leaned back, making the springs in his ancient desk chair squeal in protest.

"I'm reading the same words, over and over again. I need a break," he said aloud, letting his chair snap upright before pushing away from his desk and heading to the vending machines in the break room.

As he passed the front desk, he paused and leaned against the counter.

"Anything interesting come in, Sergeant?" he asked.

"Not really, sir. Everyone's working on the missing girl case. All I've got is a report about a stolen dog."

"Oh?"

"A woman living over by the park says her dog was snatched out of her car while she was putting away her groceries. I figure the pooch probably just jumped out and ran away, but she insisted on making a report. I'll send someone around to get her statement as soon as there's anyone available."

"I wish I knew when that might be," Ransom said. "With a missing kid, no news is definitely not good news."

"Well, at least we haven't found her body," the sergeant said.

"Give thanks for small favors, eh?" Ransom commented, and then continued on his snack run, considering whether to have chips and a coke or a candy bar.

*

Honora, still blindfolded, bound, and gagged, shifted and squirmed, trying to find a more comfortable position on her rough bed.

The air mattress had long since deflated, her limbs were numb under the bindings, and she ached all over. She repeated the Twenty-Third Psalm over and over to keep hysteria at bay.

When she heard scratching and scraping sounds overhead and the pattering of pebbles and dirt falling nearby, she froze.

A thumping sound let her know that something heavy hit the ground close by. The echoing sounds, along with the earthy smells, made her think she was being held in an underground chamber, perhaps a basement.

After a brief flash of hope that the sounds meant she was being saved, she realized rescuers would have called out to her.

Still, she sensed a new presence in the space.

She held her breath in terror and tried to control her trembling, hoping, if it were her captor, he would think she was unconscious or dead and he would go away.

When she felt the man's breath on her face, she jerked her head back in terror.

"Good. You're awake," he said in a raspy voice. "I've brought you water. I'm going to untie your wrists, so you can sit up and drink. Don't try to get away or I'll kill you."

The man's words, spoken so matter-of-factly, chilled Honora and she did as he said, letting him pull her to an awkward sitting position. He removed the gag and she gulped greedily from the plastic water bottle.

"I don't have any food for you, right now, but I'll get you some, later, if you behave. Do you need to go to the bathroom?"

Honora did, indeed, need to relieve herself, and his question both thrilled and appalled her. What was he planning to do? Surely he wasn't thinking she would use the bathroom with him there. However, if he untied her feet to take her to a restroom, maybe she could run away.

She nodded. Although no longer gagged,

she was too afraid to speak.

"Okay. I thought of that. I got you a bucket over in the corner there," he pointed, then snorted as he remembered she couldn't see the gesture.

Honora felt him grab her left wrist and wrap something rough around it.

"I'm gonna untie your legs, so you can walk over to the bucket, but I'm gonna keep this rope on you, so don't try anything stupid."

He untied her ankles and helped her stand. Putting his hands on her shoulders, he pushed her forward. She stumbled on trembling legs until her foot touched a plastic five gallon bucket and she stopped.

"What are you waiting for? I thought you had to go," he said.

Honora shook her head, hoping he would realize she wasn't about to do anything so private in front of him.

"Well, do you or don't you?" he asked angrily.

Honora stood still, her silent tears seeping beneath the blindfold.

Perhaps softened by her weeping, the man spoke more gently.

"You're shy, I guess. Okay, I'll turn around. But don't try anything. I'm bigger and stronger than you, and I've still got this rope on you...and my knife."

The mention of a knife jolted Honora into action. She arranged her clothes as modestly as possible and proceeded to take care of her needs.

"Here!" the man thrust a wad of paper towels into her free hand and, when Honora was done, pulled her back to the pallet, where he restrained her as before.

"I gotta go, now, but I'll be back. We're gonna get to know each other real good. I already know a lot about you. I've been watching you. You're a good dancer. Maybe we can dance together someday soon," he said with a chuckle.

The sound turned Honora's stomach.

He checked her bindings a last time and clamped the lid on the bucket with a snap.

Honora thought she heard the bucket clang against metal, there was a thud, like a heavy door closing, and finally the only remaining sound was the constant vibrating hum, as before.

Honora thought about what the man had said. Did he plan to keep her, indefinitely? Or only as long as she behaved, whatever that entailed? She'd felt a wave of nausea when he'd suggested dancing together and his laugh sent chills down her spine.

Lying alone in the darkness, her ears straining for sounds of his return, she tried to block thoughts of what he might have in mind for her by mentally rehearsing her dance steps for the recital. After a long time, she fell into an exhausted slumber.

*

Tillie stepped into the public library, closed her dripping umbrella, and set it on the drying rack in the lobby. She removed her rain hat, a vintage pith helmet she'd picked up on an archaeological expedition with Gerald in Northern Africa. She'd since found the headgear was as effective in keeping off the Oregon rains as the desert sun. She wore it whenever she had to be out in a downpour like the one currently splashing down beyond the library's glass doors.

Leaving the hat and her raincoat on a hook in the lobby, Tillie pushed through the doors into the main room of the library, where she paused to breathe in the delightful aroma of literature and history as she scanned the stacks and tables.

She nodded to the librarian and walked over to a table in the far corner of the room.

"Hi," she whispered.

Slim looked up from his book and smiled, pulling out a chair for Tillie to join him.

"What are you reading?" she asked and Slim held up his book to display the title of a popular mystery novel.

"What are you doing here today?" Slim asked in a low voice.

"I'm doing some research on the history of baking."

"Baking?" Slim blurted, then lowered his voice when the librarian looked over with a frown. "You are an expert baker. Why read about it?"

"I thought it would give me something to think about while I'm kneading dough, if I knew how the whole process evolved. Also, I might try my hand at an ancient recipe or two," Tillie explained.

"Aren't you afraid of stuffing too much information into that amazing brain of yours? What if you hit capacity and stuff you really need starts falling out of your ears?"

Tillie smiled indulgently at Slim's joke, saying, "You can never have too much information, that's my motto. I'm going to look for my book, now, but would you like to take me for coffee and a donut when we're through here?"

"Sure. Just give me a poke when you are ready to leave."

11

Ransom was walking back to his desk as the sergeant put down the phone.

"Sir, that was the dog lady, again."

"Did Fido come home?" Ransom asked, munching on a Snickers bar.

"No sir. Now she says she found a carving of the dog on the hood of her car when she went out to look for him. She thinks it's some sort of voodoo doll. She was pretty hysterical on the phone."

"Have we got anyone free to go take her statement and calm her down?"

"No one's come back from the various search locations. You want me to call someone off that detail?"

"No, don't bother. I'm not doing much good here, right now. Let me have the address and I'll go see her. At least, I'll get some fresh air."

*

"Was that the police? Have they found her?" Ruth Anniston asked, rushing into the kitchen where her husband was just hanging up the phone.

"No, dear. That was Aunt Laura, just seeing if we'd had any word," Howard said.

Ruth slumped onto a stool at the kitchen island with her head in her hands.

"Why don't they call? Where can she be?" she moaned.

Howard pulled her up into his arms.

"The police promised they will call, just as soon as they know anything. Why don't you take one of the pills the doctor prescribed and try to get some sleep. You tossed and turned all night."

"I can't sleep!" Ruth said, pushing him away. "When I close my eyes, I see unbearable scenes of what could be happening to Honora. How can you be so calm? Don't you care?"

Howard pulled his wife back against his

chest and stroked her hair as she sobbed.

"There, there, my darling," he murmured. "Wherever she is, our precious daughter is in the hands of God. He loves her even more than we do. We have to trust Him."

Howard gently led Ruth into the living room and eased her onto the sofa where he covered her with a crocheted blanket and sat beside her, rubbing her back until her weeping ceased .

When he saw she was asleep, he slid onto the floor beside the sofa and his shoulders began to shake with his own muffled sobs.

*

Detective Ransom perched uncomfortably on a spindly-legged antique chair, balancing his notebook on one knee.

His hostess, Mrs. Diane Dumont, sat on the chair's matching brocade-covered settee clutching the small wooden carving of a dog.

Looking at it with revulsion, she thrust the carving at Ransom, saying, "Here. You take this evil thing. I can't bear to touch it another second."

Ransom took the small wooden figure and slipped it into his pocket.

"Thank you, ma'am. I can return it to you when we no longer need it for evidence."

"I don't ever want it back! I just want my Percy, before he's used in some sort of Satanic ritual."

"We're doing what we can, Mrs. Dumont, but we don't have a lot to go on. Are you sure the dog didn't just jump out of the car?"

"Of course not! The windows were up and the doors were closed. My Percy is very smart for a Lhasa Apso, and they are known to be an intelligent breed, but even he can't manage door handles and window buttons. And he would never run away from his Mumsy."

"You're sure you didn't see anyone hanging around your car before you found the carving? And no strangers in the neighborhood?"

"I'm sure."

"I guess that's all for now, then. We'll be on the lookout for your pet, and I've notified Animal Control. I'll let you know if anything turns up."

Ransom eased himself forward and straightened up, relieved when the fragile chair remained upright and in one piece.

"I can see myself out, ma'am."

He opened the front door and swung his foot forward to step out, but froze with his foot in midair when he saw what appeared to be a ball of bloody fur on the doormat. He stepped back inside and bent down for a closer look.

Hearing Mrs. Dumont approaching, he turned and blocked her view.

"Was your dog white, ma'am?" he asked.

"Yes, I already told you that."

"Well, then, I'm afraid I've got some bad news."

12

Mimsy Waits and Laura Breem sat in the older woman's living room. The wooden statuette of a ballet dancer stood on a cocktail table between them.

"You say this was left for you at the studio, Mimsy?" Laura asked.

"It was addressed to the dance teacher, but when I got a good look at it, I thought I should show it to you."

Laura picked it up and rubbed her fingers over the wood.

"It does look a bit like Honora in one of her dance moves, I suppose. But, really, it could be any generic ballet dancer, don't you think?"

"Well, yes," Mimsy said. "I only thought it was a coincidence, what with Honora going missing, and all."

"I appreciate your good intentions, but I don't see how this could be anything except a gift to you from an anonymous admirer. Odd timing, I'll agree, but it can't have anything to do with my niece."

Mimsy nodded and stood.

"You're probably right. Guess I was just imagining things."

"Thank you, dear. We're all grasping at straws," Laura said, handing the carving to Mimsy and showing her out.

Mimsy walked next door, went into her house, and set the carving on a bookcase in the den, beside the mementos of her brief dancing career.

She stepped back to admire the effect, moved it closer to a framed program from her one-and-only professional performance, and, satisfied with the effect, went into the kitchen to microwave a couple of frozen diet meals for her dinner.

"Could it really be from her own secret admirer, as Laura suggested?" Mimsy wondered.

She liked the idea, but had to admit there wasn't a single potential candidate in her life.

*

The sun was shining the next day when Tillie trotted up the three steps to her friend Opal's door and rang the bell. While waiting, she admired a window box overflowing with crimson ivy geraniums and blue lobelia. The vibrant colors seemed to be reflected in the swirling print of Tillie's silk tunic and wide-legged palazzo pants.

In a festive mood that morning, Tillie had styled her single braid into a corona on the top of her head, adding a welcome inch to her height.

Her tote bag contained a still-warm loaf of cinnamon bread, fresh from her oven.

"Hi, Tillie!" Opal said, opening the door. "I'm so glad you could come by on such short notice."

"You said it was important. Is anything the matter?" Tillie asked, edging into her friend's small, cramped living room.

Opal spent much of her time outdoors tending to her garden and bee hives. The interior of her home got a much smaller share of her attention and reflected that fact.

Tillie moved a stack of Apiary Life magazines from the seat of an upholstered chair near the door and plopped herself down in their place, sending up a puff of dust.

"Here's some of that cinnamon bread you like," Tillie said, handing over the wrapped loaf.

"Oh, thanks," Opal replied, taking an appreciative sniff of the yeasty aroma before setting the bread atop a messy pile of unopened mail on the cluttered sideboard.

Her smile faded and she slumped down onto the sagging sofa.

"What's wrong?" Tillie asked.

"I need your advice. I think I may have some important information about Honora Anniston's disappearance, but it could be nothing. I don't want to get someone into trouble, if it's only my overwrought imagination. I just can't decide what to do. I absolutely hate indecision!"

"What's the information?" Tillie asked, leaning forward.

"I was over at Laura's yesterday evening and she told me something that triggered the ghost of an old memory. I couldn't put my finger on it at the time, but it niggled at my mind and when I awoke this morning I knew what it was," Opal said.

"Yes?" Tillie prompted.

"This happened nearly twenty years ago, you see, when I was teaching second grade here in Tillamook. I think you were still teaching in Bannoch, back then," she said and Tillie nodded.

"We had a problem with stealing in my class one year," she went on. "Little things would disappear from the children's desks and cubbies; nothing valuable, but it was disturbing, and no one knew who was doing it. During our unit about birds, we studied the magpie and its habit of taking shiny things and the children began referring to our thief as the magpie. Later, figures made from modeling clay began to appear in place of the stolen items. These sculptures were crude, but usually resembled what had been taken. I explained to the children that such habits were more in line with pack rats than magpies, but they'd become so enthralled with the idea of our thief being an actual bird that I couldn't dissuade them."

"What does all that have to do with Laura's grand-niece's disappearance?" Tillie asked.

"Laura told me Honora's dance teacher, who is Laura's next-door neighbor, brought over a wooden carving of a ballet dancer. It was left, anonymously, at the studio the morning after Honora went missing. Mimsy thought the carving looked like Honora and might have something to do with her disappearance. Laura said it was a rather good carving of a dancer, but she saw only the vaguest resemblance to the missing girl.

"It was the idea of something, in this case, some*one*, going missing and a sort of replica appearing in her place which triggered my memory," Opal concluded

"Did you ever find out who the thief in your class was?" Tillie asked.

"Well, yes. That's why I'm not sure if I should mention this to the police. The boy was seen leaving a little blue clay horse in the cubby of a girl whose pony toy had been taken. It was really a very good sculpture for a second-grader," Opal said.

"So, who was it? Does he still live around here?"

"Yes. That's the problem. What if I get him into trouble based on something he did as a small child? I'm sure he and his family would rather forget such an unfortunate episode."

"But, what if he took Honora? Don't you have to tell the authorities and let them check it out?" Tillie asked.

"I don't think I can. I know the boy's mother and she hasn't had an easy time of it. I don't think I could look her in the face, if I went to the police."

"Then tell me who it is and I'll report it. The mother doesn't know me, after all, and I can keep your name out of it," Tillie suggested.

Considering this, Opal picked up the loaf of bread and absentmindedly opened one end of the plastic wrap. Tearing off a yeasty chunk swirled with cinnamon, brown sugar and raisins, she popped it into her mouth and began to chew slowly, rather like a thoughtful cow.

"Well?" Tillie prompted.

Opal swallowed and nodded, saying, "Okay. But, for sure don't let them know where you heard about it."

"I promise," Tillie said, standing up. "Now, how about offering me some tea and a slice of that bread, toasted, with your delicious honey on it?"

*

When she returned home, Tillie grabbed a recent newspaper out of the basket beside the fireplace and carried it to the dining room table where she searched for the phone number of the missing persons tip hotline. When she found what she was looking for, she tore out the page and returned the rest of the paper to the basket.

She picked up her phone and, after considering what she was going to say, tapped in the number.

"Hello, I have some information for the officers in charge of the Honora Anniston investigation," she said, and went on to give her name and number and to relate Opal's story as if it were her own.

The clerk took down her report and thanked Tillie, saying an officer would be in touch if they needed more details.

"Well, I've done all I can, Aggie," Tillie said to the cat who had jumped onto her lap and was kneading Tillie's thighs.

Agatha purred, anticipating a comfy nap, but Tillie soon brushed the cat off and stood up, feeling restless.

She picked up her phone and pressed in

110

Opal's number as she walked into the kitchen.

"Hi, it's me," she said when Opal answered. "I called the hotline."

"You didn't mention me, did you?" Opal asked.

"Of course not. The person who answered said she would pass on the info and someone might contact me, but I didn't get the feeling she thought much of your story."

"It's probably for the best," Opal said. "Now, I can forget all about it and no harm done. Thanks so much."

Tillie leaned against the sink while the two friends chatted about plans for the next church rummage sale, a planned Senior Citizens trip to the Cape Mears Lighthouse in June, and other inconsequential matters, before Opal ended the call.

Trying to study her Braille punch cards, Tillie couldn't keep her mind on the lesson. She picked up her phone and called Slim, telling him all about Opal's story, hoping to get his perspective.

"Sounds pretty far-fetched," Slim said. "It's most likely nothing at all. Connecting a little boy who swapped stuff twenty years ago with a statue sent to the missing girl's dance teacher seems like quite a stretch. I see why Opal was reluctant to say anything."

"But what if it is the same man?" Tillie protested.

"Well, that's why you needed to tell the police, right? I think, now, you can leave it up to the professionals. They'll sort it out."

"I suppose so," Tillie said. "Thanks for letting me bounce it off you. Two heads are better than one; that's my motto."

"Your ideas are always fun to bat around. Just don't throw hard questions at me, or I'll duck," Slim quipped.

Tillie groaned at Slim's corny comment and ended the call.

13

Honora had no idea how long she'd been a prisoner. It seemed like hours and hours, but the darkness was disorienting.

Immobile and with nothing to stimulate her except an ever-present fear, she dozed off and on, waking up hungrier after each slumber.

She suffered from thirst, more even than hunger. Although she'd been given a drink when the man came, he'd crammed the cloth gag back into her mouth before leaving. The rag quickly absorbed all the moisture in her mouth.

He seemed to know a lot about her, but although Honora thought long and hard about the sound of his voice, she was certain she'd never heard it before.

Why had this man chosen her, why did he leave her alone so much, and what was he planning to do with her?

She created fantastic scenarios in her mind, trying to make sense of what was happening to her, but she couldn't think of any reasonable explanation.

The only possible motives she came up with were either pure evil or insanity, with neither option providing comfort. However, refusing to give in to the paralysis of depression, she continued to think of new games and exercises to occupy her mind, while keeping up a constant stream of silent prayers from her anguished heart.

*

The sun slipped behind the western mountains as Hope walked along the highway, sticking out her thumb at the infrequently passing cars.

Hearing a growling roar, she turned to see a pair of motorcycles approaching.

One rider, a burly, pigtailed, heavily-tattooed man in a sleeveless leather vest, pulled to the gravel shoulder in front of her. His companion, sporting a spiked dog collar and a shaved head bearing an array of scars, came to a stop behind Hope.

Without showing any outward sign, her battle senses switched into high alert and she prepared to defend herself. Letting her duffel bag slide down one arm, she slipped her other hand inside.

"Looking for a ride, little lady?" the man in front of her asked, swinging his leg over the bike and getting off.

"No thanks. It's a nice night for a walk," she replied.

He swaggered toward Hope while his buddy straddled his own motorcycle and used his feet to roll it nearer.

In the gathering dusk, Hope tensed and waited for the two to close in on her.

"You don't want to be alone tonight, do you?" Pigtail smirked. "I'll bet you'd rather have some real friendly company, wouldn't you?"

Baldy snorted a nasty laugh at his buddy's wit and rolled his bike even closer to Hope.

"No. I don't believe I would, actually," she said.

When his buddy's bike was only a couple of feet from her, Pigtail made a grab at Hope.

Before his fingers closed on her, she swung the bag, knocking him off balance, while pulling out her knife and slashing it across the motorcycle tire behind her.

She whirled around and kicked Baldy off his bike before she was grabbed by her first assailant. She twisted around, elbowing his chin and breaking his hold, then stabbed him in the arm, neatly dividing a skull tattoo into equal halves.

Pigtail howled like the swine he was and charged Hope.

She sidestepped his lunge and slashed his thigh as he passed, before turning back to Baldy, her knife raised to strike, again.

He took one look at the bloody knife, picked up his motorcycle, jumped on, and roared off, wobbling away on the bike's rapidly deflating front tire.

Seeing his accomplice abandon him and realizing he was bleeding profusely, Pigtail limped back to his bike.

"You're crazy, you bitch!" he called, and sped away with a squeal of tires and a spray of gravel.

Hope watched until they were out of sight, then picked up the duffel, wiped her knife on an old sock and shoved the weapon back into the bag, her racing heart returning to normal.

She'd walked only a few yards when a battered pickup truck pulled over. As she approached it, an older man in a cowboy hat stuck his head out the driver's side window.

"You want a ride?" he called.

Hope, seeing a bale of hay and a worn saddle in the back of the truck, looked into the rancher's weathered face and made her decision.

"Sure. Thanks. How far you headin'?" she asked, climbing in.

"Yreka. You going that far?"

"That far and beyond, but Yreka will do for now. I appreciate it."

The rancher pulled back onto the highway.

"My name's Arvil," he said.

"Hope," she replied.

"I like music while I drive, but the radio's busted, so I don't mind a bit of company. Just to stay awake, you know."

"Well, I can't sing for you, but I'm happy to provide a little conversation, Arvil," she said as they rode up the highway.

14

The sun's rays filtering through the leaves of the wisteria vine outside her bedroom window eased Tillie from sleep the next morning.

She stretched to loosen her body's kinks and rolled into a sitting position on the side of the bed before sliding her feet into fluffy slippers.

Glancing fondly at the two framed photographs on her bedside table, she blew a good morning kiss to her late husband and son and stood, taking mental inventory of her body's aches and pains, and then sank back down onto the bed.

"Come on, Tillie girl, you're *ripe and ready*, remember. A ripe peach left on the shelf will soon have a squishy bottom; that's my motto, so I'd better get a move on, isn't that right, Edgar?"

The tortoise, in his night terrarium, having heard this many times before, wisely ignored her.

Tillie shuffled into the bathroom to let a steaming shower wash away the night's lingering stiffness.

She wove a cheerful pink velvet ribbon through her braid in an attempt to counter the downward pull of arthritis on her spirits. After dressing in brightly colored yoga togs, she strode into the kitchen to prepare breakfast with a more youthful step.

Tillie toasted a slice of Old Testament sprouted-grain bread she'd baked from a recipe in her library book and slathered it with honey-sweetened Greek yogurt mixed with raw pumpkin seeds and blueberries.

She washed this down with milky strong black tea before responding to Agatha's desperate pleas and feeding the apparently starving feline.

"You poor baby! Nothing to eat except this bowlful of perfectly nice dry cat food you've ignored since yesterday! How do you survive such ill treatment?" she cooed while opening a tin of

Pampered Kitty Delights.

She moved Edgar from his terrarium on her bedroom dresser to the roomier one she called his "play pen" under a dining room window.

He gazed up at her solemnly, his silent version of Agatha's "feed me now!" command, and Tillie quickly obeyed before grabbing her yoga things and dashing out to catch the bus.

*

Tillie arrived early for her yoga class, in plenty of time to limber up before the others arrived.

Working through the morning's routine, she felt her joints becoming more flexible with each exercise and was in fine fettle by the time her first students appeared.

"Good morning, Olivette!" she called, seeing her new friend enter. "Did you remember our shopping date?"

"Yes, but are you sure you want to do this?" Olivette replied, as soon as she was close enough not to be overheard by the other women who were unrolling their mats. "I don't really need any new clothes."

Tillie looked pointedly at Olivette's gray sweats with her eyebrows arched and Olivette giggled.

"We'll get you sorted out and you'll be surprised at how it lifts your spirits. Happy colors for a happy life; that's my motto," Tillie said.

Olivette took her place on the floor, Tillie turned on her CD, and the class began.

*

Squeals of laughter bubbled from the dressing rooms in one of Tillamook's nicest dress shops. The girlish sounds were followed by oohs of pleasure as Olivette pirouetted before the mirror in a cerise jersey knit dress with a softly flowing knee length skirt.

"That's the one! We must get that one, too," Tillie declared. "You look beautiful."

"I've never worn this color, but it does flatter

me a bit, doesn't it?" Olivette said.

"You flatter it, you mean. You are glowing. Do you want to wear it home? Kendall will be swept off his feet."

At mention of her husband, Olivette sobered.

"If he recognizes me, you mean," she said.

"Not at all. He'll be knocked for a loop by the vision of this beautiful woman, whether he knows you are his wife or not. And if not, then let him court you all over again," Tillie suggested.

"Really?"

"Sure. What harm would it do? You could have fun. Play-acting uses your imagination to help keep your brain healthy, too. It is awfully important to add some fun to your days when you are a caregiver, you know. "

"I've had more fun today than I can remember, Tillie. Thank you so much! You must let me pay for at least some of these beautiful clothes, though," Olivette said.

"Nope. That wasn't the deal. I've had as much fun as you, so I'm happy to pay for my entertainment. I've sometimes paid more for a single concert ticket and enjoyed it far less."

Burdened with an assortment of shopping bags, the two dropped into a coffee shop for tea and lemon pie.

Olivette put her fork across her empty plate and leaned back to sip her tea, sighing with satisfaction.

"This has been the nicest day, Tillie. Thank you," she said, admiring the sleeve of the new royal purple silk shirt she had decided to wear home with slim gray wool slacks.

"Seeing you like this is a treat for me. A good deed is its own reward, that's my motto. You're more than welcome."

"I'm afraid I've been letting myself indulge in a bit of depression," Olivette said.

"It's easy to do, especially when you're in

difficult circumstances."

"But, I'm a Christian! I should be content in all circumstances, just as the Apostle Paul was. If my faith were stronger, I wouldn't give in to self-pity."

"I know your husband was a minister and that you know your Bible, dear, but you should also know our faith doesn't make us immune to our emotions," Tillie said. "That's not anywhere in the Scriptures."

"Give thanks in all things, is there, though," Olivette said.

"Yes, and gratitude helps us overcome the pits of despair, but it's a constant struggle. We need to use all the tools of our faith; gratitude, trust, prayer, reading the Word, and we must add to those tools with some God-given, common sense, practical steps. Enrolling in my exercise class was one of those steps and going out for some fun is another one. Even indulging in a treat, now and then, helps. Don't be too hard on yourself when you get sad. It's natural and necessary to grieve for what you've lost."

"Thanks for your wise words. I feel so much more hopeful."

"There's not much point in living as long as I have, without learning a few lessons along the way, I always say," Tillie laughed. "Now, let's plan our excursion to the Quilt Museum."

*

At his desk, sifting through a stack of recent reports from the tip line, Detective Ransom noticed a familiar name and sat up straighter. It was the record of a call from a Matilda Thistlethwaite. He felt sure there couldn't be two women in the area with that unusual name.

As Ransom read the report, he thought back to his first encounter with Mrs. T., when he'd been investigating a cold-case murder in Bannoch a few years earlier. She had provided information about the victim which eventually led them to the perpetrator.

Ransom also remembered the delectable baked goods she'd served on his visits to her home. His stomach growled and he picked up his phone to arrange a visit, deciding it was a good time to check out her story.

*

Before dinner that evening, Olivette tried on her new cerise dress. She'd begun to feel guilty for allowing Tillie to splurge on her that afternoon, but when she stood before her mirror wearing the dress, she felt the same rush of joy she'd experienced in the dress shop.

She was twirling before the mirror, feeling rather young, when Kendall walked into their room.

"Oh, I beg your pardon, miss!" he said, beginning to back out of the room in confusion.

"Wait! Don't go," Olivette called. "How do you like my new dress?"

He paused with a frown before stepping back into the room, extending his hand.

"I'm afraid we haven't been introduced. My name is Kendall Vernon. And you are?"

Just as she'd feared, her husband didn't recognize her. Remembering Tillie's suggestion, she decided to give it a try. She shook his hand.

"I'm Olivette. I'm pleased to meet you."

"Olivia, that is a pretty name," Kendall said, misunderstanding the name due to his bad hearing.

Olivette didn't correct him.

"Thank you," she said.

Taking a deep breath, she went on, "What do you do for a living?"

"I'm a seminary student, now, but one day I will be a minister of the Gospel. Do you know Jesus?"

Olivette walked with her husband into the sitting room where she let him lead her down the Roman road to salvation and their 'courtship' began.

15

Two days later, the first time their schedules allowed for the visit, Ransom parked at the curb in front of Tillie's cottage, jumped out, and paused to admire her garden. The riot of colorful plants and flowers had grown even more lush since his last visit and Ransom smiled when he observed several additions to her bizarre collection of garden gnomes.

He stepped onto the porch, avoiding hanging baskets of flowers, and ducking under the colorful wind chimes and sun catchers.

When Mrs. T. responded to his knock, her cherubic face peering at him through the sidelight transported him mentally back to their first meeting, when he'd first noticed her resemblance to one of her smiling gnomes.

"Detective Ransom! How nice to see you

again," Tillie cried as she opened the door. "Please come in."

Ransom admired the skillful watercolor paintings adorning the entry hall and remembered these were Tillie's own creations.

She ushered him into her tastefully decorated parlor where he was gratified to see a tray piled high with iced cinnamon rolls and a pot of coffee awaiting them on a low lacquered table in front of the sofa.

He sat down and immediately drew his notebook from his pocket, but Tillie stopped him, insisting they should eat before getting down to the business at hand.

Ransom readily agreed.

She served the refreshments and the two chatted amiably, catching up with each other's' life.

When the tray of rolls was significantly diminished, Ransom took a last swallow of the excellent coffee and leaned back with a sigh.

"I suppose I'd better get to work, now. I am

on the clock, after all," he said. "I've got the record of your call, of course, but do you mind just telling me what you called about, again?"

Tillie gave Ransom the particulars of the story, once again omitting Opal's name.

"So, did you ever find out who your classroom thief was?" he asked.

"Yes, we did, and I believe he still lives in the area. That's why we thought I should call and report it," Tillie replied, giving Ransom the thief's name.

"We?" he asked, writing the name in his notebook.

"Oh, uh, yes. I shared the story with a friend before making up my mind to call."

"I guess that's everything, then, Mrs. T. Thanks for the information and for the delicious cinnamon rolls. When I tell Sergeant Forester I was here today, he's going to be sorry he wasn't able to join me. He still goes on and on about your baking skills and tries to think of excuses for us to come and interview you again."

"You boys don't need an excuse to drop in, John. Why don't I wrap up these leftovers for you to take back to share with him? He's such a nice young man," Tillie said, taking the tray into the kitchen.

Ransom followed her, leaning against the counter and admiring the modern, efficiently appointed kitchen still redolent of cinnamon and yeast from her earlier baking.

Tillie filled a plastic container with the remaining rolls and handed it to Ransom.

"See that Sergeant Forester gets his share, now," she admonished him with a knowing twinkle in her eye.

"Yes, ma'am," Ransom said. "Thanks, again."

When the detective was gone, Tillie looked at the clock and decided there was still time for her regular visit to the Golden Memories assisted living facility.

She popped Edgar into his comfy travel case, along with the treats the residents liked to feed him, slipped into a warm tangerine sweater and bright yellow knit cap, grabbed her purse, and set out for the bus stop on the corner.

*

Slapping the dust from her jeans with her weather-beaten straw cowboy hat, Hope walked into Jefferson's Roadhouse on Main Street in the small California border town of Yreka. She detoured to the restrooms to wash up, and then hitched herself onto a red vinyl stool at the lunch counter, leaning her duffel bag at her feet.

"What can I get you, honey?" the waitress asked, pouring coffee into a cup.

"The biggest, juiciest burger you've got and a plate of steak fries. And iced tea with lemon," Hope said.

"You new in town?" the waitress asked, noting down the order.

"Just passing through on my way to the coast. I've got a craving to dip my toes into the ocean at Cannon Beach."

"Mighty cold up there on the Oregon beaches this time of year. You'll freeze your tootsies. You should head down south around Santa Barbara way if you want to get into the surf."

When Hope just smiled, the waitress walked away to fill her order.

The trip had gone okay, so far, other than her unexpected workout with the bikers, but the one ride Hope could catch had come only as far as Yreka. She hoped her next hitch might take her at least to Grants Pass.

She could walk the whole way, if need be, but she'd as soon ride as wear out shoe leather, any day. After eating, she planned to stick out her thumb beside the northbound freeway on-ramp and wait for a friendly long-haul trucker to pick her up.

16

In the cold darkness, Honora once again heard scraping sounds coming from above.

She'd recognized the near-constant humming noise as the approach and departure of vehicle traffic on a nearby roadway. She supposed when the sound was loudest and most constant, like now, it must be during the day and when the sound died down was night.

"I'm back, see? Did ya miss me? I told ya I'd bring you something to eat. Sorry it took so long," her captor said after jumping down into her prison cell.

Honora cringed away from the sound of his voice, but soon felt his weight leaning against her pallet.

"I'm gonna untie your legs and one hand, so you can sit up and eat. Now don't go getting any funny ideas.. I've still got my knife."

When her legs and left arm were freed, Honora lifted her hand to her blindfold.

"Stop that!" he said, slapping her hand.

"You leave that alone. I'm gonna take your gag off, so you can eat, and I'll leave it off this time, if you behave yourself like a lady."

Honora was even more terrified after he'd slapped her, until she recalled that in TV shows, whenever the kidnappers let the victim see their face, it meant they were going to be killed. If this man was protecting his identity, it might mean he was planning to let her live.

She nodded her head to let him know she would obey and he pulled the rag from her mouth.

Honora's whole body tingled and ached from being immobilized and her mouth was dry and nasty-tasting. She stretched her jaws to restore circulation and tried to moisten her tongue with saliva.

Observing her maneuvers, her captor

grabbed a bottle of water, opened it and thrust it into her hand. She grasped it and drank greedily, choking from gulping the water too quickly.

He took the empty bottle from her hand, replacing it with a spoon.

She felt him set a pan or bowl in her lap and waited, afraid of being slapped, again.

"Go ahead. It's good. It's pot roast and mashed potatoes. Go on, eat!"

Clumsily, at first, then with more assurance, Honora ate her first meal since before her capture. Despite the circumstances, it was delicious.

When her spoon scrapped the bowl and came up empty, the man took the spoon and bowl from her, slipping them into a plastic bag.

"You can use the bucket, now. Swing yourself over to this side of the bed and I'll switch your arms, so you can reach it."

Honora obeyed, hoping her acquiescence would keep her alive.

Once necessities were attended to, she

returned to sit on the pallet.

"That's it. You're getting the hang of things. Now, I don't want to have to tie you down, again. I know that's not good for your circulation, and you being a dancer, you need your circulation, right?"

Honora remembered he'd mentioned knowing all about her on his last visit. Despite what he'd said the last time he'd visited, she'd been hoping her attack was random. It seemed worse, somehow, thinking she had somehow enticed this man into attacking her.

Her mouth dropped open as confirmation of having been stalked hit home.

"Don't you go screaming, now, or I'll put that gag back!" he warned.

"I, uh, I won't," she rasped after clearing her throat. "Please don't put the gag back."

"You're polite. I like that. I kind of knew you would be," he said. "If you stay nice and polite, we are gonna get along really great, but you gotta behave."

138

"I will," she whispered.

"Good. Now, I gotta go, but even though you agreed to be nice, I can't trust you, not just yet. So, I can't leave you loose. I've been thinking about it and I figured it out. You might get your ropes off if I leave your hand free, so I got this chain and lock. It's sort of heavy, but it will keep you here, where you belong, whenever I have to be gone."

He wrapped the thick chain tightly around Honora's waist, fastening it with a padlock, then attached the other end of the chain to a metal pipe. She could hear the clang of metal against metal and the rasp of a lock snicking shut before he untied her other arm.

Honora wanted to snatch off her blindfold and attack her captor, but she was too weak.

"There. That should hold you," he said as he moved out of her reach and gathered up the bag and bucket.

She heard him go up the ladder and empty the bucket, then jump back down.

139

"I'm going now. But I'll be back and you will never know when I'm coming, so behave. And don't take off your blindfold. Not ever."

His feet hit the rungs of the ladder, there was a heavy bang and Honora was alone.

She grabbed the cloth covering her eyes and pulled it down, but the room was pitch black, she could see nothing.

Where in the world was she?

*

Tillie rapped gently on the door of the Golden Memories long-term care wing resident's room and went in, greeting her old friend with a smile.

"Up to a visit, Dottie?" she asked.

When ninety-six-year-old, Dottie Gruginski lifted her head from the pillow and nodded, Tillie took Edgar from his cage and rested him on the bed. The old woman reached out a gnarled hand and caressed the tortoise.

"How's the old man?" Dottie asked.

140

"Slim's fine," Tillie replied, then said with a grin, "Or did you mean Edgar?"

"You know I did," Dottie said. "But I'm glad to know Slim is well, too. He's a darling man. Sit down and tell me all about your latest adventures. When you go, I'd like you to mail that stack of cards on the table for me."

Although bedridden, Dottie had an active ministry. She was often heard to say, "Since the Lord hasn't taken me, yet, he still has work for me to do."

Dottie's current ministry was two-fold; intercessory prayer and sending cards of encouragement to those for whom she prayed. The daughter of missionaries, Dottie's whole life was a testimony. Time with Dottie was the highlight of these visits for Tillie. Even Edgar seemed more content in her presence.

Tillie picked up the stack of cards and noticed the top one was addressed to the Annistons.

"My heart goes out to these poor parents," she said.

"The Annistons? Yes, these are trying times for them, and for their daughter, as well," Dottie said.

"So, you don't go along with the theory that she's beyond suffering and has fallen victim of that serial killer?"

"When I prayed for the family, I received a feeling of peace. Of course, Honora and her parents are believers, so for her to be with the Lord is to be at peace, but I felt peace for her parents, too, as though their trial will not last much longer."

"I hope that's true. I don't think the Coastal Killer is the one responsible for her disappearance, either. It's just a feeling I have, but my intuition is right, more often than not," Tillie said.

Tillie and Dottie chatted as Edgar climbed slowly over the reclining woman's blankets. After praying together, Tillie took Edgar and the cards and left her dear friend to rest.

She and Edgar were finishing up their rounds of the residents' rooms when Tillie encountered Olivette and Kendall in the hallway.

"Hi," Tillie greeted them.

"Good afternoon, ma'am," Kendall responded gallantly. "I don't believe we've met. I'm Pastor Vernon. Are you a first time visitor here at the Reformed Church?"

"That's right, Pastor," Tillie replied, going along with his delusion, and introducing herself, as she did on each visit.

Olivette stepped forward and Kendall put his hand on her arm to present her to Tillie.

"I'd like you to meet my fiancé, Olivia," he said.

"Fiancé? How delightful!" Tillie exclaimed. "When's the wedding?"

"All in good time," Kendall said, then pointed to the tortoise. "What's that?"

"This is my pet tortoise, Edgar. I brought him out for a visit today. Would you like to give him a treat?"

Seeming to forget Olivette, Kendall became engrossed with giving Edgar a treat, and then, noticing an empty wheelchair sitting in the hallway, climbed into it and began to shout for his dinner.

A nearby attendant responded quickly and began to push him toward the cafeteria.

"I'll see he eats and bring him back to your apartment, Mrs. Vernon," the aide said to Olivette as they passed.

"Thank you," she replied, and then turned to Tillie, "Can we sit in the lounge for few minutes before you go?"

"Of course. I want to hear all about your engagement," Tillie said with a twinkle.

"That's your fault," Olivette said when they were settled in the lounge.

"Oh, how's that?" Tillie asked.

"I took your advice. When Kendall saw me all decked out in my colorful clothes, he didn't

144

know me. He actually flirted with me, so I went along with it. Now we're engaged."

"True love will out, I always say!" Tillie said. "No matter what his memory is like, Kendall recognizes you as his soul mate."

"It has been awfully fun," Olivette admitted. "A few times our 'courtship' has sparked his memory of the early days, too. Of course, it is bittersweet when he drifts away again, as you saw. And when he speaks to me, I never know if he's addressing the real me, the fiancé he calls Olivia, or a stranger."

"Would you rather you hadn't played along?" Tillie asked. "I'd hate to think my suggestion has made your life more difficult."

"Oh, no! It's an unexpected blessing to be able to fall in love all over again, but I must confess to feeling a little guilty for enjoying myself. It seems as though I'm tricking him."

"What makes him happier, you playing along with his confusion, or trying to correct him?"

"He gets angry and frightened when I try to explain his confusion, no matter how gentle I am. I suppose this way is better, but what I really want is for everything to be normal again."

"When you can't have what you want, enjoy whatever blessings come your way is my motto. You've got nothing to be ashamed of," Tillie said.

Olivette stood up, saying, "Thanks for letting me natter on. I feel better. I shall simply learn to be content in this present circumstance. These precious moments may be gone all too soon."

"That's my girl," Tillie said, standing and giving Olivette a quick hug. "We never know what tomorrow will bring. Wring every drop of joy from the present moment is my motto, or one of them."

17

Back at his desk, John Ransom completed a report on his visit with Tillie and filed it, along with his notes on the killing of Mrs. Dumont's dog, into a folder labeled "Dead Ends" and slipped it into the back of the case file box.

The aroma of Tillie's delicious cinnamon rolls reached him and he looked longingly at the plastic container sitting atop the file cabinet across the room. The interview hadn't been a complete waste of time, after all.

He'd been surprised by that story Mrs. T. told him. She was usually pretty sharp for her age, but there was no way he could pursue a story about classroom thefts from decades earlier. He couldn't see any real connection to the Anniston girl's disappearance, either. He'd leave himself open to accusations of harassment if he even questioned the man Mrs. T. suspected.

Giving in to temptation, Ransom got up and grabbed a cinnamon roll, telling himself Forester would never know one was missing, but as he picked it up the telephone rang. He reluctantly dropped the pastry back into the container and snapped the lid shut.

"Ransom," he answered.

He listened intently, making notes, before saying, "That's just the break we need. I should be at the hospital in Medford in a few hours. See you there."

The cinnamon rolls forgotten, he hurried to the day sergeant's desk.

"Who's available to go with me overnight to Medford?" he asked. "The Coastal Killer just tried to grab another girl down near the California border, but this one got away. I'm going down to interview her at the hospital. Could be she can tell us something about the Anniston girl."

*

In the long, dreary hours of darkness, Honora tentatively explored everything within reach of the chain.

When her extended fingers encountered something warm and furry, she recoiled with a scream.

Defying her captor's warning, she continued to scream for help until her throat was raw. Exhausted, she finally had to accept that there was no one outside who could hear her.

She slumped back onto the cot to consider what she'd learned about her prison and decided it was a concrete enclosure, probably underground, with a hard cement floor. Pipes ran along the wall above her bed. From the way her screams had echoed, she sensed the space was not large.

Her captor had left water bottles and the plastic bucket within her reach, a gesture which made her feel extraordinarily grateful, under the circumstances.

After exploring the boundaries of her cell, she tried to exercise her legs, now that she was no longer afraid of crashing into the walls. However, leaps and kicks were awkward encumbered as she was by the heavy chain and she soon gave up the effort.

The empty hours dragged on and Honora's initial terror ebbed to a dull anxiety, leaving her in a state of lassitude from emotional tension and physical inactivity.

Despite her fears, Honora almost looked forward to her kidnapper's next visit, just to break the monotony.

She kept her ears pricked for the sounds of his return, when she would need to pull her blindfold back down over her eyes.

Waves of horror sometimes surged into her consciousness and at those moments she fought hysteria by forcing herself to think past her current ordeal to the day when she would dance free.

*

Inside Twinkle Toes Dance Studio the rehearsal music played as usual, the young dancers posed, leaped, and twirled, as usual, and their teacher, Mimsy, tried to lead her students with her usual enthusiasm, but something was definitely missing.

"Very nice, girls. Take a break," she called out, switching off the music and slumping on a stool.

Without her star pupil, their performance in the charity program was going to be a disappointment. The girls' parents would applaud with gusto, but she couldn't expect that rest of the audience to be impressed.

With Honora at center stage, the failings of the rest of the troupe faded into the background, becoming a colorful blur supporting her talent. None of the other dancers could fill that gap and Mimsy had been forced to simplify the choreography to the beginner's level, more suitable for toddlers in butterfly costumes than her class of advanced teens.

Perhaps she had focused too much on Honora. Maybe that's why the others were having so much trouble learning their parts.

She had several more classes before the performance to make it up to them.

Hopping down from the stool, she clapped her hands to bring the class to attention.

"Let's take it from the top, ladies."

"Aren't we through for today?" Samantha asked. "My feet hurt."

"We have only a few more rehearsals to get this right, so we need to go through the entire program again before end of class today," Mimsy said.

"Why bother?" another student asked. "We are never going to do any good without Honora."

The other dancers nodded or commented in agreement.

"We can't think that way," Mimsy said. "We

must give our very best performance…we'll do it for Honora. I think we should dedicate our dancing to her memory."

"Don't you think she's ever coming back?" Shantee asked in a small voice.

Mimsy flushed and tried to correct her mistake.

"Sure, she's coming back. That was just a slip of the tongue I meant to say we should do the performance in her honor, if she doesn't return in time," she said and turned on the music, saying, "Places, ladies!"

As the students tried to stay together and move gracefully to the music, Mimsy kept an encouraging smile on her face, while in her heart she mourned the loss of her favorite student.

If Honora were still alive, she believed she would have been found by now.

*

Tillie felt better after leaving Opal's suspicions in the capable hands of Detective

Ransom. He would follow up on the incident, so they needn't worry about it any longer.

Tillie's heart was light as she prepared to attend a late afternoon performance Slim and his silly band were putting on at another elder care facility. Many of these residents were in need of more assistance than Golden Memories could provide.

Slim had gone on ahead, so Tillie took the bus and would walk the last two blocks from the bus stop to the rest home.

She loved to walk and always wore comfortable shoes, choosing them both for support of her aging feet and for their colorful designs.

Today's leather Mary Jane's boasted a tooled and painted floral pattern coordinating perfectly with her buttery yellow knit shift. She'd topped it with an antique paisley shawl for warmth.

She stepped off the bus with a jaunty step, enjoying the mild sunshine after a foggy morning, and looking forward to seeing what shenanigans

Slim would come up with this time.

Entering the care center, she immediately pulled a rosemary-scented handkerchief from her tote, holding it delicately to her nose until she'd acclimated to the geriatric hospital's pervasive aroma.

The staff did what they could to keep the residents and the facility clean and wholesome, but no amount of disinfectant could completely disguise the tell-tale ambiance of old age and incontinence.

Tillie always came prepared.

In the activity room, many residents were already seated around tables awaiting the performance or dozing in their wheelchairs.

Tillie didn't see Slim or any of his band, so she took a seat in one of the folding chairs arrayed along the wall and waited for the show to begin.

Esther, the activity director, saw her and hurried over.

"Mrs. T.! I'm glad you could come. The

residents are so excited about this new group. You've seen them before, haven't you?"

"Oh, yes. I've had that privilege. They are a unique act, for sure," Tillie said.

"Mr. Bottoms is a dear man, and such a character! Our people just love him. I can't wait to see what he's got for us today," Esther said, then walked up to the front of the room when she saw Slim poke his head out of a side door.

Esther exchanged a few words with Slim and then clapped for attention before introducing the day's entertainment.

"I know we all want to give a rousing welcome to our guests, Slim Bottoms and the Wrinkly Keesters Kazoo Band."

"I want to watch my TV shows!" a high-pitched voice quavered over the smattering of applause. "What am I doing here?"

Esther scurried over to the upset woman and squatted down next to her wheelchair, speaking softly.

Slim and his band marched in, enthusiastically blowing a variety of individualized variations on When the Saints Go Marching In. They followed Slim, weaving like a conga line in and out of the tables, before forming up at the front of the room with a final dissonant squawk.

Slim turned to smile at his audience, bowed and gestured for his "orchestra" to take a bow, and then announced their second number.

There were a few weak claps and the band launched into Mack the Knife, while performing hilariously uncoordinated dance moves.

Following a few more numbers, Slim asked the audience for requests and that's when the attendees came to life, asking for old favorite hymns and tunes from their youth.

When Slim noticed his Keesters were flagging, he announced the final number, Goodnight Ladies, and the performance ended to loud applause and good natured heckling

Tillie waited in the lobby for Slim to disburse his band and escape his many admirers. She was sitting, leafing through an outdated Modern Living magazine, when she noticed the cleaner from her Braille class come into the lobby, accompanied by her shy son. Tillie wondered if Detective Ransom had already questioned them.

The two seemed surprised to see the crowd milling around, but squeezed through the clusters of visitors until they were blocked between a wheelchair and a large woman speaking loudly to the chair's occupant.

They stopped beside Tillie's chair to wait until this obstacle moved on.

"Quite a crowd today, Marjie," Tillie said, looking up.

Startled, Mrs. Whipple bumped back into her son, causing him to drop the package he'd been carrying.

"Oh, hello," she said to Tillie. "There aren't usually so many visitors here."

"It's for the special performance today. Slim Bottoms and his Wrinkly Keesters put on quite a show for the residents and their guests. Are you here to visit a family member?" Tillie asked.

"My mother," she said.

Danny Whipple had retrieved his bundle and was examining it.

"Is it broken?" his mother asked. "Let me see."

Danny handed it over and she held up the carving of a dolphin, checking for any damage.

"That's lovely," Tillie said.

"My Danny made it for his Nana," Mrs. Whipple replied.

"You have a real talent for carving, Danny," Tillie addressed the young man, who shrugged.

"He's always been good with his hands. Right now he's working on something really special for his new girlfriend, but he won't let me see it," Mrs. Whipple said.

Tillie opened her mouth to ask about this

girlfriend.

"Hi, sorry to keep you waiting," Slim said, arriving at her side.

"Do you know the Whipples?" she asked, turning to introduce the pair just as they disappeared down the hallway.

"Who?" Slim asked, looking around.

Tillie got up, taking the arm Slim offered.

On the way to Slim's car she explained about the introverted Whipples, reminding him Danny was the long-ago thieving 'magpie' in Opal's class.

Slim drove across town to the local homeless shelter, where they were both signed up to help their church serve that day's free dinner.

"Marjie Whipple didn't seem too upset. I wonder if she's been interviewed, yet," Tillie said. "I hope John Ransom isn't going to delay too long."

"Maybe he's already talked to her and there wasn't anything to rile her up," Slim said, turning into the homeless shelter parking lot. He narrowly missed a heavily laden shopping cart pushed by a toothless woman who was hurrying toward the line now forming for admittance.

"I certainly hope so. Although, the more I see of that Danny, the more I don't like. He seems more sly than shy, to my mind," Tillie said.

Slim parked near the service entrance and they entered the shelter kitchen, calling greetings to their fellow servers.

Thoughts of the Whipples were soon driven from Tillie's mind as she donned an apron and plastic gloves, moved to her assigned serving station, and prepared to greet the hungry diners with a smile and large helpings of hot, tasty food.

"A friendly smile is sweeter than a spoonful of sugar, that's my motto," she said softly.

18

Alerted by the sounds of his approach, Honora was sitting primly on the cot with her blindfold in place the next time her kidnapper dropped down the ladder.

She'd been nervously preparing a little speech for this moment and hoped she wasn't about to make her situation even worse.

"Hello," she croaked, then cleared her throat and continued. "I appreciate the things you've brought me to eat and drink and all, but I'd like to ask you for something else. I've tried to behave, like you said."

"Yeah? What do you want? I'm not letting you go, you know," he said, sounding suspicious.

"That's not it. I'm just so bored when you aren't here. I've got nothing to do. I just sit in the dark. I wondered if maybe you could leave me a candle or a flashlight or lantern or something, for when I'm alone," Honora said. "Then maybe you could get me something to read, or maybe my schoolbooks. I'm probably falling behind in my classes, already. I promise I will put my blindfold back on when you come to see me."

The man didn't speak and Honora was afraid she'd asked for too much. She wished she could see his face, so she'd know how he was reacting. If he was angry, would he hurt her?

"I'm not gonna give you a candle. You could cause a fire, or something, and you might hit me with a flashlight or a lantern, if you could see where I am. Here, eat your dinner," he said, thrusting the plastic container into her lap.

Honora was disappointed, but when he didn't lash out at her for asking, she relaxed a bit and began to eat.

The man emptied her bucket and put fresh water bottles beside her cot.

"I'm putting extra water here, and a couple

of towels, so you can wash. You should keep clean."

When the food was eaten, he took the empty container and plastic spoon and prepared to leave.

"I'll think about what you asked. I can't give you those things, but I'll think about what I can do. I want you to get to like it here with me. I got you a dog to keep you company, before, but it bit me, so I took it back."

After he'd gone, Honora pushed up the blindfold and jumped to her feet. She pulled as hard as she could against the chain, the links grinding into her ribs, but no matter how she strained, she wasn't able to reach the ladder. With a final painful lunge, her fingernails scrapped against the metal, but she couldn't grasp it.

Honora slumped to the floor and began to weep in frustration.

Sometime later, she was roused by the sound of the door being lifted.

Sunlight shone down. Honora blinked and

tried to memorize everything she could see before pulling her blindfold back into place. Her quick glance took in metal shelves along one wall and a battered plastic chair. A card table supported a lantern and bottles of water. Faded posters dotted the walls, as in a child's hideaway.

"Here, I gotcha something," her captor said, putting a hard plastic shape into her hands.

"What is it?" Honora asked.

"A battery radio. Now you can listen to music. Maybe even practice your dancing," he replied, guiding her fingers around the knob and turning it on.

At first there was only static, but when he pulled up the antenna and fiddled with the dials, music filled the room.

"Oh!" Honora gasped. "Thank you!"

"Sure. I told you I'd be good to you if you behaved. You been really good, so you should have a treat. Someday, when you get over wanting to escape, we'll have lots of fun. You'll see. I gotta go, now. I might be gone for a while."

He jerked forward, planted an awkward kiss on Honora's face, then dashed up the ladder and slammed the hatch.

Honora's initial delight at having the radio to make her solitude more bearable was instantly chilled by the kiss and what it might portend.

*

The following morning, Tillie was in her painting studio on the back porch washing out her brushes when the phone rang. She dried her hands on her paint-spattered smock and pulled her phone from its pocket.

"Hello?" she said.

"Hello, Tillie? This is Olivette. I hope I'm not interrupting something important. If you are busy, I can call back later."

"I'm never too busy to chat with you," Tillie said, settling onto an old church pew she used as a bench. "What's up?"

"A friend of mine from Bannoch, really a

friend of a friend, but I know her, too, is going to be at the Book Nook bookstore signing her new book this afternoon and I thought you might like to come with me and meet her."

"What's her name? Will I have read any of her books?" Tillie asked.

"She's my friend, Bunny Banks, but she writes under a pen name, Leveline Davis. She writes thrillers. Her last book, *Death Stalks*, was on a best seller list, I believe. You might have heard of it."

"I think Slim was reading that book, until it scared him, anyway. He told me he could only finish reading it in broad daylight with a bodyguard standing by, but he was probably joking," Tillie said. "I'd love to meet the author. Maybe I can get a signed copy of her new book for Slim."

"Wonderful! I'll come by for you about three o'clock. See you then."

*

Olivette's author friend finished reading aloud from her latest novel and asked the small gathering if they had anything they'd like to ask her.

Tillie raised her hand.

"Do you ever find it depressing to write about such dark subjects?" she asked.

"Good question," Bunny replied. "In my books, the bad guys never get away with their evil deeds. If they sometimes got away with it, like in the real world, I suppose it probably would get me down, though. Anyone else?"

After a smattering of questions about the author's life and writing processes, she sat at a table and the fans queued up to have their books signed.

When she finished, Bunny joined Olivette and Tillie for a private chat in the cozy seating area in a corner of the bookshop.

*

As Olivette drove them home after the book signing, Tillie read the jacket flap on the book she'd purchased for Slim.

"It was nice of your friend to spend time with us after her presentation, Olivette. She's led a fascinating life. I'm surprised she doesn't write about some of her own experiences."

"I suppose Bunny has been through a lot. Maybe she finds it too personal to share with strangers, though."

"It's comforting to know she hasn't had first-hand experiences like the ones in her books, anyway. This new one is about a serial killer truck driver who finds his victims along his route. It sounds like that Coastal Killer we've been reading about in the news. It might make for exciting fiction, but I hate to think there are actually such evil people in the world."

Olivette pulled up at the curb in front of Tillie's home.

"Would you like to come in for a cup of tea?" Tillie asked.

"I'd better not. I've been away from Kendall

too long, already. Thanks for joining me today."

Tillie took the book inside, fixed herself a cup of tea, curled up in her favorite chair, and began to read.

She finished the novel before going to bed that night. Thoughts about the story filled her mind long after she'd turned out her light.

The killer in the book was so similar to the news reports about the one who'd been haunting the coast for the past few years, it seemed as though the author had him in mind when writing.

Cold-blooded killers, whether fictional or all too real, were hard to comprehend. Profilers and psychologists gave explanations about what prompted such people to kill for sport, but Tillie felt the true cause was much simpler; pure evil.

She couldn't believe a person like that had been right here in Tillamook, walking among them, and had snatched Honora without leaving a trace.

Unreasonably, she imagined she would have felt such a malevolent presence, like a Jedi master feeling a disturbance in The Force.

Tillie chuckled softly at this flight of fancy, chasing away her uneasy feelings. With a sigh, she rolled over and drifted off to sleep.

19

"**Uhn,**" the man groaned in the darkness and rolled over into an oily puddle under the rear wheels of his rig.

"What did that skank hit me with?" he groaned, looking around and crawling out from under the truck.

Passing headlights swept across the nearby weedy verge and glinted on metal, revealing the handle of a lug wrench from his toolbox. It should have been in his cab, not lying in a clump of weeds. He picked it up and felt stickiness on the handle. Looking closely, he saw it was coated with blood. His blood.

He touched the bump on the back of his head and winced.

Swearing, he climbed back into the truck, started the engine and pulled onto the highway,

172

wasting no time shifting into top speed.

The girl was long gone, but she would be running to the cops. It wouldn't be long before she brought them back here, looking for him. He didn't know how long he'd been knocked out, but there wasn't a moment to lose.

He kicked himself for making a stupid mistake.

Already headed for LA, he'd been in Yreka getting a bite to eat when he'd spotted the tall redhead beside the northbound on-ramp. He'd decided to take another little detour and pick her up.

He got on the Interstate, now, and headed north until he could return to the coast road, where he would turn south again.

The girl would tell the cops he was heading north when he picked her up, so the police might not think to look for him on the coast highway heading south.

He couldn't risk traveling the Interstate,

now, though. The cops would have a description of him and his rig. They might even put out a multi-state alert, if the witch got his truck number.

He should have never stopped for the stupid cow, but the glow from his earlier encounters had begun to wear off. When he saw her standing beside the road with her thumb out, he'd felt that irresistible urge flare up again, stronger than ever.

He'd been careless and now he would be driving through the night without a break, fleeing from the cops.

After all these years without a hint of suspicion, he'd gotten sloppy.

He would have to off-load the trailer the first second he could and lose himself in Southern California, or maybe go on down to Mexico until things cooled off.

None of his victims had ever fought back like the red-haired she-devil. It was like she wasn't even afraid of him. He'd been sure he could overpower her, but when she got a hand free, she clawed his eyes, he'd recoiled in pain, and she jumped out of the cab.

He'd quickly caught her again, but he hadn't seen her grab that wrench.

His head continued to throb where she'd bashed him, but he hadn't even checked to see how much damage she'd done; just wiped the blood out of his eyes with his dirty handkerchief. He couldn't take time for first aid.

Staying on secondary highways throughout the chilly night, few cars passed, but their headlight beams revealed beads of sweat glistening on his face and neck. Fear tailgated his rig down the highway. Traveling through the mountains, he almost missed a curve, but he didn't dare slow down.

The dashboard gauge showed his gas was getting low. He would be running on fumes when he reached the isolated station he was aiming for. He probably wouldn't run into any other customers there. He could only hope they wouldn't have been alerted to be on the lookout for him.

It wouldn't take long to fill the tank, get cleaned up, and be back on the road, as long as nothing went wrong.

The gas gauge read empty when he coasted up to the diesel pump at the tiny station on the edge of a small, dusty town in California's Central Valley.

After many hours of driving without seeing a single trooper or patrol car, he was beginning to relax.

His good luck held as the gas station attendant, a scrawny, bored teenager, took his money without even looking up from the game he was playing on his cell phone.

The trickiest part of his escape plan was going to be offloading and dropping off the trailer once he hit LA. If the cops had his license number, they might be able to figure out who he was hauling for on this run and be waiting for him at the loading dock.

As he neared his destination, he decided delivering his load was too risky. He took a detour off the tangle of Los Angeles freeways and abandoned his rig in an industrial park a few miles from his apartment. He planned to walk there, grab the money he'd stashed for an emergency, and head for the border.

*

Detective Ransom made good time driving to Medford. He and Officer Minch checked in with the local authorities, found a cheap motel, and grabbed some burgers at a local Red Robin before driving to the hospital.

It was almost seven o'clock in the evening when they approached the nurses' station to ask about the Coastal Killer's recent victim.

Ransom flashed his credentials for the charge nurse, a heavyset woman in her late fifties with frizzy iron gray hair.

"Is Hope Masterson able to answer a few questions?" he asked.

177

"Her condition is stable, but it is rather late, and the local police already interviewed her," the nurse replied, frowning.

"I've talked to them, but I have some questions about a missing persons case we're working on. We hope Miss Masterson may be able to shed some light on our girl's fate. We think she may have been picked up by the same perp."

"Let me see if she feels up to seeing you," the nurse said, disappearing into one of the intensive care rooms nearby. The room was dark and the blinds on the observation window into the hallway were drawn.

She soon returned, saying, "She hasn't been able to fall asleep, yet, and she is willing to see you. But please keep it short. She needs her rest."

The officers thanked the nurse and walked to the room she'd indicated.

Hope Masterson lay back on the pillow, her face almost as pale as the bed linens, except for the deep purple bruises on her cheek and jaw. She was a tall girl and seemed well-muscled, which probably accounted for her escape, but she hadn't gotten away without injury. As well as the bruises to her face, she had been slashed on one shoulder and broken her left wrist.

"Thank you for seeing us, Miss Masterson. I'm Detective Ransom from Tillamook and this is Officer Minch. The nurse said you would answer a few questions for us."

Hope nodded.

"I've read the report of your interview with the Medford police, so I won't go over what you were already asked. We are looking for a young girl from Tillamook who's been missing for a few days, now, and we're hoping you might be able to help us."

"You think that creep got her?" Hope asked, anger flashing in her eyes.

"That's what we are trying to check out, yes," Ransom said. "Did you see anything of a slim, blond, seventeen-year-old? Or did your attacker mention the name Honora?"

"I'm sorry. I didn't see anyone else in his truck. He didn't talk about anyone. If he got her, she's probably done for. That man's a filthy monster."

"Did he indicate where he'd come from before he picked you up?"

"He said he was on an LA to Seattle run, like I told the other cops."

"Of course. Sorry. We're grasping at straws here, I'm afraid," Ransom said.

"Did the guy say anything about a dancer?" Minch asked.

"A dancer? No. Like I said, he didn't talk about much until he started to attack me, then the things he said were disgusting. I'd rather not think about that. I should have known better and picked up on the pervert vibes before I ever climbed into his cab. I won't make that mistake, again."

Hope turned her face away, saying, "I'm tired. Is that all you want? I really don't think I can help you."

"Of course. Thank you for seeing us. We won't bother you, anymore, now.. But if you think of anything, please give me a call. I'll leave my card," Ransom said, sliding his card onto the tray table.

Hope nodded, waving them away with a limp hand, and the disappointed officers went back to the motel.

Ransom called the office with his report for the Tillamook task force, letting them know the trip had been unproductive.

"I'm bringing a copy of the Medford case file back with me, though, in case there is anything worthwhile in there. See you tomorrow before noon," he said and ended the call.

Flopping down on the sagging and lumpy motel bed, he muttered a frustrated curse and punched the hard pillow before turning out the light and trying to get to sleep.

20

Tillie met Slim at their favorite coffee shop the next morning, a rare sunny late-March day.

"Spring will be here before we know it," Slim said, looking out the window at the bright scene. "I expect it's always springtime in Heaven."

"I hope we'll have seasons in Heaven," Tillie replied. "I enjoy each one in turn and love the variety."

"I expect we'll both find out, soon enough," Slim said, looking glum.

"What's the matter?" Tillie asked. "Are you feeling unwell?"

"No. Just the usual aches and pains, those badges of honor I've earned for surviving all these years. Only I've been thinking about how nice it will be to escape this world's troubles when the time comes. I ran into Howard Anniston yesterday.

The poor man is a wreck. Just thinking about what he and Ruth are going through makes leaving this world's ills behind look pretty good."

"The pain they are in from not knowing what their daughter might be going through or where she is…I can't imagine how they go on. I've got them in my prayers, but things like this are always so hard to understand," Tillie said. "Somehow it all fits into God's eternal plan, even so."

"In this world we shall have trouble," Slim said, nodding.

"Oh, I almost forgot," Tillie said, picking up her tote bag. "This is for you."

Surprised, Slim took the book and looked at it, smiling.

"Leveline Davis's new book! How about that," he opened the cover. "And it's signed for me, too. How'd you manage that?"

"She's a friend of a friend. She lives part of the year in Bannoch, just down the coast. Anyway, she had a book signing here in town yesterday," Tillie said.

"Well, thanks. I really liked her last book."

"I have to confess I read this one before giving it to you. It's a good story, if you like that sort of thing," Tillie said.

"Oh, I do," Slim said.

"I think I prefer gentler fiction. I had all sorts of silly thoughts after finishing that book."

"Nightmares?" he asked.

"Not really. Anyway, I hope you enjoy the book. I think I'd better get back home, now. I've got bread rising and it should be about ready."

*

In the darkness and isolation of her prison, Honora kept the radio on for company, hoping to hear news reports about her disappearance, but her heart sank when the radio's batteries died following an update stating there were no new leads.

When the radio went silent, the solitude

184

suddenly seemed more intense and even more difficult to bear.

Slumped on the cot, trying to ease the pain from the chain links rubbing against her bruised and tender flesh, she wondered if everyone had given up.

Well, not everyone, she reminded herself. Even if the police gave up, Honora knew her parents would keep searching until they found her, one way or another.

Sickened to think of her mother and dad being called to identify her moldering remains, she jumped up and screamed for help, standing on her cot and pounding her fists on the rough concrete ceiling until the heavy chain dragged her down and she collapsed back onto the pallet, weeping.

21

It was raining when Olivette arrived at Tillie's house the next day. She dashed from her car to the door, holding her handbag over her head.

"Come in, come in!" Tillie said, balancing the purse on the umbrella stand to dry and pulling her friend through the hallway into the parlor where a tall, thin woman dressed in flannel and denim stood.

"Olivette, I would like you to meet my dear friend, Opal. She's an avid weaver, so I invited her to join us today."

"Hi," Opal said. "I hope you don't mind me horning in on your party."

"I'm pleased to meet you," Olivette replied. "I'm happy you can join us."

"Of course, you are!" Tillie said. "Opal's weaving club meets at the quilt museum, so she will be able to give us the cook's tour."

The ladies donned raincoats and Tillie grabbed a couple of umbrellas to protect them from the sudden downpour as they hurried to Olivette's sedan.

"Oh, this is charming!" Olivette exclaimed when she parked in front of the white-painted school building housing the museum.

"The school is well over one hundred years old," Opal said. "When it was donated, the abandoned schoolhouse had blackberries sprouting through the floors and birds flying in and out the holes in the ceiling. You'd never know it, now."

"It's been a museum since the early 1990's," Tillie added.

When they went in, they headed first to the West Room where there were spinning wheels and several looms with works in progress, along with displays of hand-woven textiles, tatting, beading and knitting.

"If you are interested, Olivette, lessons can be arranged by appointment and are usually held on Fridays. Opal can help you with that," Tillie said.

The three ladies wandered from room to room, with Opal explaining everything for Olivette. They ended their tour in the gift shop, where Olivette selected a calendar featuring award-winning quilts.

"What about one of these?" Opal asked, picking up a primitive-looking rag doll. "My group makes them from one of my ideas."

Olivette took the doll which bore a tag saying, "old-age voodoo doll" and began to read out the words embroidered on the body, "Pot belly, arthritis, insomnia, bunions, gas?" she laughed.

"Sure. Any of that stuff starts bothering you and you can stick a pin in it!" Opal said.

Olivette added the doll to her purchases and the three ladies went back out into the rain.

J. B. Hawker

"Come back to my place for a hot drink. I made scones this morning," Tillie said as they rode through the wet streets.

"Sounds good," Opal replied.

"I'm not sure I should leave Kendall much longer," Olivette said, pulling up in front of Tillie's place.

"He is being well cared for at Golden Memories, dear. Taking a few moments for yourself won't hurt," Tillie said. "Now, let's get inside while the rain's let up a bit."

Leaving dripping umbrellas and jackets in the hall, the ladies gathered in Tillie's bright kitchen while she made coffee and served the scones.

A bright bunch of daffodils in the center of the blue-checked tablecloth added a touch of sunshine as she placed a platter of scones on the table, along with butter, jam and honey.

"Be sure to try the honey, Olivette," Tillie urged. "It's from Opal's bees and it is delicious!"

Olivette turned to Opal in surprise.

"You have bee hives as well as spinning your own yarn and weaving?" she asked. "Do you churn your own butter, too?"

"Well, truth to tell, I have done, back when me and my husband lived on the farm. We raised sheep, but we had a couple of cows, too. I taught school, so Bud did most of the farming. After he passed, the farm was too much for me, so I moved into town."

Olivette picked up a scone, spread it with butter and honey, and took a bite as Opal talked.

"Why, this is excellent!" she exclaimed.

"Thanks. The bees do all the work, though. If you'd like to follow me to my place when we finally get out of Tillie's hair, I'd be happy to show you my hives," Opal said.

"I'd like that," Olivette replied. "I've never seen a beehive, up close...they aren't dangerous, are they?"

"Nah," Opal replied, adding, "You aren't

allergic, are you?"

"Well, that's settled then," Tillie said. "I just knew you two would get along. Old friends and new friends make the best friends. That's my motto."

The ladies enjoyed their snack and Opal and Olivette stood to leave.

"Don't you want to come, too, Tillie?" Olivette asked. "It doesn't seem right to go off like this and leave you to clean up our mess."

"What mess?" Tillie asked, stacking their plates. "You two go on. I've seen the bees, the chickens, and Opal's massive garden more times than I can count."

"Thanks for the eats," Opal said to Tillie, before jerking her head toward the door to urge Olivette to head out.

Olivette gave Tillie a quick hug and let Opal herd her out.

Tillie stood at the front door waving at her friends as they drove away.

"That's what I call a good day's work," she said to Agatha, who had come out of hiding when the guests left.

"Come on, Aggie, you can help me clear up the mess in the kitchen."

*

The rain had stopped and the sky was clearing by the time Olivette stepped down Opal's back porch steps into the large garden.

Rows and rows of loamy soil displayed early green shoots identified by seed packets on stakes. These were side-by-side with tomato cages and bean poles supporting growing vines. Easy access to these vegetable plants was provided on stepping stones set amongst beds of bright yellow marigolds planted to ward off garden pests.

Beyond the garden, Olivette could see chickens pecking at the ground in front of a little shed with a tiny ramp leading to its open door. Several square white wooden beehives stood off to one side of the wire chicken enclosure.

"Why this is wonderful!" Olivette exclaimed. "It's like a piece of the countryside, right here in town."

"That's what I was aiming for," Opal smiled. "I call this my city farm. I've got the bees, the chickens, and the crops. No sheep or cows, but it's enough to keep me busy."

They wandered between the rows of the vegetable garden, with Opal picking off caterpillars and pulling up any weed brave enough to show its head, and tossing these treats to the chickens.

Arriving at the beehives, Opal donned her beekeeper's bonnet and gloves to show Olivette the inner workings of the hives.

Olivette remained at a distance, but was fascinated by the industrious insects.

The clucking of the hens and the humming of the hives wove a soothing cocoon around Olivette, filling her with a sense of peace and well-being.

"Could you use some eggs?" Opal asked,

breaking the spell.

"Oh, yes!" Olivette said. "We eat many of our meals in the cafeteria at Golden Memories, but we do have a kitchenette in our apartment and I like to cook, now and then. I'd love some fresh eggs from chickens I've actually met."

Opal entered the chicken coop through a door on the backside of the building and Olivette followed, stepping carefully through the feathers and other detritus covering the floor.

"Off you go, Sheila!" Opal said to a sitting hen, lifting her off her nesting box gently, to reveal a clutch of eggs.

Opal took a basket from the shelf over the nests, put the eggs inside, and continued addressing the hen, "Sorry, old girl, but you wouldn't get anything from these beauties, no matter how long you sat on 'em."

"It makes me a bit sad, now and again, disappointing the broody hens. I'm thinking about bringing in a rooster for a time and seeing what these girls can get up to. It's about time for some new faces in the flock," Opal commented as she led Olivette back toward the house.

"You don't have a rooster, now?" Olivette asked.

"I haven't liked to take the chance of annoying the neighbors. They've been good about not complaining about the hens. You see, we aren't exactly zoned for agriculture. Still, they might not mind a rooster, if I promised he'd just be visiting and not a permanent fixture."

*

"Slim," Tillie spoke into the phone from her perch on a kitchen stool. "I called to talk to John Ransom this morning, just to see how his interview with the Whipples went, and guess what I found out?"

"How many guesses do I get?" Slim asked. "Have they finally discovered what happened to Jimmy Hoffa?"

"Don't be so silly! Detective Ransom wasn't

even there. Apparently he'd hared off after a suspect clear down in Medford, when he should be looking closer to home. I did get to speak with that nice Sergeant Forester, though. He couldn't thank me enough for the cinnamon rolls I sent over; he just went on and on about how much he loved them. He must not get much home baking. I'll need to take him a batch of cookies one day soon. Anyway, he told me the police aren't pursuing the Whipple connection! What are we going to do?"

"Uh, nothing?" Slim offered.

"Of course not! We need to find out if that boy has anything to do with poor Honora's disappearance. No one else is going to do it."

"I'd like to help put your mind to rest, Tillie dear, but just how do we do that? We aren't detectives, after all, and we have no authority to interrogate this young man or his mother, even if we had the know-how."

"But, we can keep an eye on him and see where he goes, can't we?" she asked. "That can't do any harm and we might learn something helpful."

"I guess that's okay. I'm always up for a road trip. Only we better keep a low profile. We don't want to get into trouble for stalking the poor kid."

"We'll be careful, of course. Anyway, old folks are practically invisible to young people. I'm surprised the military doesn't use gray hair and wrinkles as camouflage. Invisibility is an old woman's superpower, I always say. I don't think we need to worry about him noticing us."

"Even so, you'd better wear something more subtle than your usual garb, just to be on the safe side; no neon colors or wild feather boas."

"Oh, you!" Tillie laughed, hanging up the phone and beginning to make plans.

22

Slim pulled his car up at the curb and tooted the horn for Tillie early the next morning. It was the first day of their surveillance on Danny Whipple.

Tillie had obtained the Whipple address from Opal, without revealing her plans.

Slim smiled to see Tillie trotting down the steps dressed for serious detective work in a black trench coat and matching fedora.

"Whatcha got there?" Slim asked as she opened the car door and slid a large hamper onto the backseat.

"Stakeout supplies, of course," she replied, getting into the front seat and clicking her seatbelt. "We need drinks and snacks to keep us alert, after all. This could be a long day."

"Sounds good," Slim nodded and started the car.

"I hope it doesn't take too long before we discover something, though," Tillie said after they'd traveled a few blocks.

"Why's that?" Slim asked.

"I have a bagpipe lesson this evening. It's only my second lesson and I'd hate to miss it."

"Bagpipes!" Slim cried, coming to a sudden stop in the middle of the road, before recovering with a glance in the rear view mirror, and resuming the car's forward progress.

"Why in God's Creation would you want to learn to play the bagpipes?"

"To keep my mind agile, of course. The more types of skills a person can learn, the longer the mind will stay sharp. You know all about my regimen of cerebral calisthenics. As I've told you more than once, I must keep adding to the variety of things I learn, if I want to grow new brain cells and stay sharp. If you can't even remember that, I think you should join me for some of my classes."

"Oh, right. Sorry. That must have slipped

my mind," Slim said, rolling his eyes. "The Whipple place is on the next block. Where do you want to set up our stake out?"

"Just behind that motor home parked catty corner across the street, I think. The big rhododendron bush hanging over the sidewalk will help to camouflage us. For once the hideous mottled green paint job on your car will serve a good purpose."

"Now, no slurs about ol' Betsy. You mustn't hurt her feelings. She gets us around just fine," Slim said, patting the dashboard with affection. "Let's see what goodies you've got in that hamper."

Tillie unfastened her seatbelt, got up onto her knees, and reached over the seat into the back to open the hamper.

She leaned a bit too far, and Slim began to laugh at the sight of Tillie's short legs kicking to prevent her precipitous descent into the back. He caught her around the waist and pulled her upright.

"I thought I lost you for a minute there," he laughed.

Tillie gave him a sheepish glance before straightening her clothes and holding up a plastic container.

"I baked some of those granola cookies you like," she said, pulling off the lid.

"All right!" Slim said, putting the container on the seat between them and taking a cookie.

"I've got apples and carrot sticks, too, and a thermos of coffee. There are sandwiches for our lunch, later."

"You'd better let me get the other things when we're ready for them," Slim said with a grin.

Tillie pulled a large pair of binoculars from her tote bag, slipped the strap over her head, and began to scan the street, trying to get a clear fix on the Whipple home.

"See anything interesting?" Slim asked around a mouthful of chewy oats, nuts and raisins.

"I can't get these silly things to focus," Tillie

complained, handing the field glasses to Slim.

He lifted them to his eyes and Tillie, who still had the cord around her neck, was pulled against him, knocking the cookies off the seat. Slim lunged to save the cookies and the two friends slid off the car's bench seat, coming to rest entangled in the binocular strap and covered in cookie crumbs.

They blinked and began to laugh as they pulled themselves back up onto the seat.

"We are quite a pair of sleuths, Tillie my girl," Slim chuckled, gathering up the larger pieces of cookie.

"I don't need these silly things, anyway," she said, pulling the strap over her head.

She looked out toward the Whipple house and came to attention.

"Slim! There he is! Our target is on the move. We've got to follow him," she urged.

"Okay, okay. Calm down. We've got to take it easy and stay back. He's on foot, so he isn't about to get away from us."

The two amateur detectives buckled up, Slim started the car's engine, and the chase was on.

*

"Where did he go?" Tillie said, standing in the middle of the bicycle path in the park with her hands on her hips.

"I saw him come into the park here, but it took me too long to park the car. I'm sorry, Tillie. I'm afraid we've lost him," Slim said.

Tillie paced back and forth, muttering to herself.

"I guess we'd better go on home for today," Slim said. "At least you won't be late for your squawk bag lessons."

"No," Tillie said, walking back toward the road. "He came in here, so maybe he will come back this way, too. We can wait for him in the car."

"But, remember that big backpack he wore. That thing was stuffed. He might be on an overnight camp out, for all we know."

"Unlikely. He doesn't look the outdoor type

to me," Tillie said. "However, we will set a time limit. If he doesn't show up in a couple of hours, we'll give up for today. Okay?"

"Okay. That will give us time to eat that tasty lunch you packed," Slim said, walking more quickly toward the car.

They'd scarcely finished their picnic when Tillie saw Danny emerge from the park and head back toward his home.

"Look!" she cried. "Get ready to follow him."

Slim wiped his hands on a napkin, tossed it into the back and started the car.

"Is that the way your mother taught you to pick up after yourself?" Tillie chastised him, as she gathered up the remnants of the meal and tucked them neatly into the hamper before buckling her seatbelt.

"Don't lose him, now," she added.

"I'm on it," Slim replied. "Say, do you see his backpack? When we saw him before it was crammed full, but now it hangs on his back like a deflated basketball. I wonder what he's done with all his stuff."

"There is a laundromat on the other side of the park," Tillie said. "Do you suppose he was just doing his laundry?"

"Nah. You don't use a public laundry, so you might not know it, but if you don't want your clothes stolen or dumped on the floor, you gotta watch 'em like a hawk. If he'd been doing his washing, that backpack would be full of the clean clothes. He'd never go off and leave 'em."

Danny returned home without showing any awareness he was being followed and Slim took Tillie home.

"I want to do this again tomorrow, Slim, if you have the time. I want to find out what's up with his backpack and what he was doing in the park," Tillie said.

Slim carried the empty hamper into the kitchen and scratched Agatha behind the ears when she jumped up onto the counter to check it out.

"Thanks, Slim," Tillie said, lifting the cat back onto the floor. "Here, take the rest of these cookies. They should be better than the broken ones on the floor of your car."

Slim took the bag of cookies, stuck one into his mouth, gave Tillie a quick hug and left.

"He's a good man, Aggie, but he sure can eat!" she commented on her way into her room to change out of her detective clothes.

*

"Great news!" John Ransom cried, putting the phone down.

"What's up," Sergeant Forester asked.

"The Identikit sketch the Masterson woman gave the Medford police got a hit. Someone recognized the man as a former employee of a trucking company. California authorities are going to his last known address and his current employer is being interviewed about his schedule of deliveries. When they match up to his victims, he's going to have some explaining to do."

"Will we be able to link him to the Anniston girl, do you think, so we can get in on the investigation?"

"I've asked to be kept in the loop and my contact in Medford said he'd try to get me in on the interviews when they have him in custody. Oh, man, I never thought we'd get this close."

"Will we be able to tie him to our case without a body?" Forester asked.

"We can try. You know, some of these guys start spilling their guts once they get caught. Let's hope he'll confess and lead us to where he buried the poor girl. I hate to think of her family never getting closure."

"Do you want me to call off all the remaining search teams, now?" Forester asked.

"I think so. It's been almost a week with nothing new turning up. Once the perp starts talking, we'll have a better idea of where to look for our evidence. Teams out tramping around will only risk compromising the forensics," Ransom said. "Prepare a press release saying we have new information and the search is being suspended. I guess I'd better go brace the Annistons."

23

In a rundown Los Angeles suburb, the FBI investigative unit, wearing protective gear, swarmed over a cramped, squalid apartment, opening drawers and poking into every cupboard. Fingerprint dust covered the hard surfaces and agents carried out bags of evidence vacuumed from the soft coverings. The rooms had been luminoled for blood trace.

A female agent carrying a cardboard shoe box approached her supervisor.

"Look at this," she said, opening the box.

The lead agent took the box and sifted through its contents.

"Costume jewelry, the kind teens and young women wear. Not the usual adornment for a long-haul trucker. If we can connect any of these pieces to the victims, we'll have this creep cold. Good work."

*

Back at the FBI field office, a special agent forced her way through a gaggle of reporters and rode the elevator to the guarded interrogation suite where the suspect was being held.

Special Agent Harmony Billings approached this interview with mixed feelings. She had reviewed the files on the victims and the suspect and was confident they had the right man, if one could call such a creature a man. However, sitting calmly across the table from such evil would take all of her self-control. Worse yet, she must get him to talk by appearing to be sympathetic.

In her mid-thirties, medium tall, with medium brown hair and eyes, Harmony was a mid-level agent, eager to break out of the middle of the pack and advance her career and this was just the sort of high-profile case to give her a needed boost.

She'd have to fight against her revulsion if she wanted to get inside this killer's head and get a confession.

She paused outside the door, squared her shoulders, and smoothed down her blazer jacket before nodding to the guard and entering the room.

Alfonse Avino, AKA the Coastal Killer, a swarthy man in his fifties with a bandage on his head, sat hunched forward in the chair flexing his tattooed biceps and making his shackles rattle.

He glared at Agent Billings when she walked in and looked her up and down, doing his best to intimidate her.

"Mr. Avino, I am Special Agent Billings. Do you know why you are under arrest?"

"Cause you need a date for the prom, I guess," Avino sneered.

Harmony ignored the taunt, saying, "You were positively identified by one of your victims as the man who attacked her, Mr. Avino. In the commission of your crime you took this woman across state lines. That is why the Bureau was called in. You're accused of a very serious Federal offense.

There is the possibility of special circumstances being added which could make you eligible for the death penalty. Has that been explained to you?"

Harmony saw fear flash in Avino's eyes before he looked away.

"I want a lawyer," he muttered.

"Very well," she said.

Disappointed and relieved, in almost equal parts, she left the interview room and took a deep cleansing breath of fresh air.

Now the dance would begin with the lawyers and the DA. Harmony hoped there would be enough corroborating evidence to link the man to his other crimes. Even more than she wanted to advance her career, she wanted this guy off the streets for as long as possible.

*

Tillie decided to drop in on Olivette and see how she and Kendall were doing.

Entering the lobby of Golden Memories, she saw Olivette sitting in the lobby with a well-dressed couple who appeared to be in their late forties.

"Tillie!" Olivette called out. "Come and meet my friends."

"Hello," Tillie said, walking over with a smile.

"Tillie, I'd like you to meet the Reverend Doctor Tyrone Evans and his wife, Eskaletha, my good friends from Bannoch."

The couple stood and reached out to Tillie, expressing their pleasure as they all shook hands.

Eskaletha, tall and elegant in a buttery yellow suede suit, with her ebony hair piled high on her head, reminded Tillie of the busts of Nefertiti she'd seen in the British Museum. Physically, Tyrone was a fitting match for his wife; tall, distinguished, and with eyes full of intelligence and kindness.

"Dr. Evans is the senior pastor at the Bannoch African Methodist Episcopal Church. Eskaletha and I were in a pastor's wives support group together for many years," Olivette said.

"We were just talking about the local teen who is missing," Olivette said. "One of our friends in the support group was kidnapped a few years ago, so we know what this girl's friends and family are going through."

"We will pray for a happy ending to this disappearance like we had. Our friend was found alive and well," Eskaletha said. "It was a painful experience, but it deepened all our friendships. We will soon be leaving our beloved Bannoch, though. We stopped in today to let Olivette know we have been called to the Springfield AME Church."

"That's quite a large congregation, isn't it?" Tillie asked.

"Yes. It's an honor to be asked to lead their ministry," Tyrone said. "We will miss the fellowship in Bannoch, though."

Tillie sat for a short time with Olivette and her friends as they chatted about Bannoch and the Evans's hopes for their new ministry.

"It was lovely to meet you," she said to her new friends. "I'd better be getting along. I only came by to see how Kendall is doing, Olivette. Is today a good day?"

"He knew me when I greeted him today. Or, at least I think he did," Tyrone said. "He knew I was a fellow clergyman, at any rate."

"Oh, I think he knew you," Olivette said. "He often speaks of the friendship you've shared over the years. He hasn't forgotten you."

"One day, when we pass into Glory, our minds will be fully restored and we can experience even closer relationships," Eskaletha said. "That thought comforts me as we prepare to move away from all our friends."

"Springfield isn't Australia, after all. You will be able to visit and keep in touch, even on this side of Heaven," Tillie said.

"Of course," Eskaletha smiled. "Good-byes are just so grim, I get a bit carried away."

"I know you will find many wonderful new

friends in your congregation and in the Springfield community. I hope I get to see you, again, whenever you pass this way, too," Tillie said, hugging Olivette and saying goodbye to them all.

*

"Have you found anything?" Mr. Anniston asked Detective Ransom.

The two men sat across from each other in the Annistons' living room. Mrs. Anniston was in the kitchen making coffee.

"Let's wait until your wife is here, Anniston," Ransom said, alarming Honora's father by his solemn tone.

"Oh, no! Please, don't tell me you've found her body," he moaned.

Mrs. Anniston carried in the tray of coffee in time to hear her husband's words and paled.

Ransom jumped up, removed the tray from her trembling hands, and set it on the low cocktail table.

"Please sit down, Mrs. Anniston. We have

not found your daughter, but there has been a development in the case."

"Tell us!" Mr. Anniston pleaded.

"You will be hearing on the news later today that we are suspending the search for your daughter," Ransom began and Mrs. Anniston cried out in protest.

"Let me explain," he said.

"Why would you stop the search, if you haven't found her?" Mr. Anniston asked.

"We have some new information leading us to believe your daughter has been a victim of the man being referred to as the Coastal Killer," he said, noting the parents clutch each other's hands as he spoke. "We now know the identity of a man suspected of being responsible for the series of abductions and we are close to having him in custody. We are hoping he will be able to lead us to your daughter," he went on, pointedly not saying the word 'body'. "With his information, we will be able to resume the search more effectively."

Honora's mother slumped against her husband. Tears trickled down her soft cheeks, leaving trails in her face powder.

Mr. Anniston folded forward, holding his head in his hands, and uttering anguished sounds.

"I'm so sorry for your loss." Ransom murmured and stood to make his escape. "We will be in touch with you as soon as we have any news. Thanks for the coffee."

Back in his car, Ransom slammed his fist against the steering wheel, feeling ashamed and frustrated. Delivering that blow to these good people left a bitter taste in his mouth. It was a part of his job he hated.

After a visit like this he often thought longingly about taking early retirement and finding a job flipping hamburgers.

Forcibly turning his thoughts from the anguished couple inside the house, he focused on the prospect of catching and punishing the man who was truly responsible for all their pain.

218

24

The following morning, Tillie was outfitted in camouflage print hiking gear topped by her ancient pith helmet secured with a green chiffon scarf. This interesting ensemble was her notion of appropriate garb for tracking prey through the wilderness.

She'd packed their provisions in an old canvas rucksack, another souvenir of her late husband's archaeological expeditions.

"You planning an assault on the pyramids, Tillie?" Slim asked when he saw her.

Tillie gave him a withering look, handed him the rucksack and buckled up.

"I realize Danny may not go out today, and even if he does, he might not go to the park, but my intuition says he will, and I want to be prepared. We mustn't lose him this time"

Slim parked around the corner from

Danny's house, on the route he'd taken before. If he went any other direction, they would miss him, but today was invested in testing Tillie's intuition. All other options were on hold.

Two hours passed with no sight of Danny.

Tillie tried to practice reading her Braille cards while Slim worked Sudoku puzzles.

"It's no use," Tillie said.

"You want to go home?"

"No, I don't mean that. He'll show up, you'll see. I was talking about these cards. I'm afraid I've lost the sensitivity in my fingertips I need to learn Braille. The more I practice, the more the little bumps blend together. I've waited too late to learn this particular skill."

"Maybe you could use sandpaper on your fingers like old-timey safe crackers?" Slim suggested. He hated to see Tillie discouraged.

She laughed, brightening at Slim's concern.

"No matter. Nobody can defeat time forever, that's my motto. I've got the bagpipes to work on, now, anyway. Oh, look! Here he comes. Scrunch down a little," she said, sliding down below the windows.

Slim leaned over and whispered, "I don't think you need to bother. Your head hardly clears the dash."

They straightened up in time to see Danny walk around the corner toward the same park entrance he'd used the day before. Once again, his backpack was stuffed full.

"We can be pretty sure which way he's heading, now. Let's get into the park ahead of him," Tillie urged.

Slim drove an alternate route, as she suggested, arriving well ahead of the young man.

"Where should we hide?" he asked as they walked into the park.

"The path forks about fifty yards from here. Let's wait there," Tillie suggested.

The two spry octogenarians hunkered down behind a clump of shrubbery in a gully beside the path and waited for Whipple to pass.

By the time he appeared on the path, elderly muscles and sinews were getting stiff and as Danny moved past, Slim's knees gave out, throwing him forward through the bushes.

"Hey!" Danny cried, jumping back. "Who are you?"

Slim straightened up, brushing himself off and trying to gather his wits.

"Why'd you jump out at me? What were you doing?" Danny challenged.

Remaining out of sight, Tillie scooted backwards out of the brush, walked around to another part of the path and approached the men.

"Oh, there you are, dear!" she called out, hurrying up to Slim. "Are you okay? I just spied a yellow-billed grackle and you missed it."

She looked at Danny, feigning surprise, and gushed, "Why, you are Danny Whipple, aren't you? I met you and your lovely mother the other day. How's your grandmother doing? Did she like your dolphin carving?"

Whipple looked between Slim and Tillie in confusion.

"My dear friend, Slim, and I were birdwatching and got separated. Do you do any birdwatching, Danny?"

"Nah. I've got better things to do," Danny grumbled, turning away and leaving.

When he was gone, Tillie walked to a nearby bench and sat down to catch her breath. Slim joined her, shaking his head.

"Sorry! My legs locked up, crouched down like we were. Do you think he suspects anything?"

"Who knows? Young people expect us old codgers to behave oddly. He's probably forgotten we were ever here...unless he really is up to something. Did he seem nervous to you?"

"At first, sure, but I'm thinking you'd be nervous, too, if a giant praying mantis leaped out of the bushes at your feet."

"Praying mantis?" Tillie chuckled.

"I'm just imagining what I must've looked like, springing out at him," Slim said.

"Hmmm," she said, looking at him with eyes squinted. "I can just about see the resemblance, at that."

"So, what do we do now? Can we catch up to him, do you think?"

"Let's go home. We can use a soak in a hot bath after our misadventures."

"Is that an invitation? I thought you'd never fall under my spell," Slim teased, wiggling his eyebrows and twirling an imaginary cigar, ala Groucho Marx.

Tillie swatted his arm playfully, and then let him help her to her feet for the short walk back to the car.

*

Stepping out from behind a large oak tree, Danny Whipple watched them leave. He'd heard enough to confirm his suspicions.

Those two batty old people had been

following him and thought he might be up to something.

Why? They couldn't know where he was really going, so what did they suspect him of?

He walked on, considering what he should do about them. He couldn't let them mess up everything.

*

"I tell you, John, that boy is up to something!" Tillie said. "He's too shifty."

"I've got a lot of respect for your intuition, Mrs. T., as you know, but I can't base my investigation on it."

Tillie sat in the visitor's chair beside Detective Ransom's desk. At his words, she leaned forward, nearly slipping off the wooden surface. Putting one crimson sneaker against the desk, she wriggled back onto the chair and pleaded, "Can't you at least check out his whereabouts at the time the Anniston girl disappeared?"

"I'm sorry, but we just don't have the

manpower," Ransom said. "Besides, and I shouldn't be telling you this, we are pretty close to catching the guy we believe is actually responsible."

Letting her feet slide to the floor, Tillie stood, leaning her hands on the desk.

"Who is it?"

"I can't share the details, but you can rest assured he will soon be apprehended, now the FBI is on the case."

"Why the FBI?" Tillie asked.

"They often get involved with a kidnapping, but in this case, our suspect also crossed state lines to commit his crimes."

"His crimes? Don't tell me you think this so-called Coastal Killer is responsible for Honora's disappearance?"

"I'm afraid I'm not at liberty to discuss the details of an on-going investigation, even with you. I've already said more than I should have."

Ransom stood, indicating the interview was

over.

Tillie was frustrated and annoyed at her friend's stubbornness, but she'd used all her arguments.

"Thank you for taking the time to talk with me, John. I believe you are following a red herring, but I wish you luck. Right or wrong, the most important thing is to find Honora."

*

Tillie's phone began to ring as she opened her front door.

Digging in her tote, she stepped inside and pushed the door closed with one hip.

"Hello?" she said, plopping down on a chair.

"Hello, is this Matilda Thistlethwaite?" the caller inquired.

"Yes."

"Oh, good! Mrs. Thistlethwaite, this is Constance Wilson, the sub-coordinator for the Tillamook School District."

"How are you, Constance? I haven't heard

from you since I gave up substitute teaching," Tillie responded.

"That's why I'm calling. We are desperate and I've got a huge favor to ask."

"What is it ?"

"You know Mr. Hanson's class at the middle school, right?"

"Yes. That's the class for difficult students, isn't it?"

"Right. It is the last step before expulsion for most of these kids, but Mr. Hanson manages to keep them under control, most of the time, somehow. Anyway, he has to be out tomorrow on a family emergency and I can't find a sub willing to fill in," Constance said.

"Are you asking me to take the class? I haven't taught in years," Tillie said.

"But you were always able to keep a class in line, no matter how difficult, and I don't know who else to ask. Won't you consider filling in tomorrow? It will be only for the one day. Please!"

"Constance, you know I stopped subbing when I got fed up with all the new education policies and ridiculous regulations. I can't teach that way, and I won't."

"It's only for one day…"

"If I agree to come in tomorrow, it has to be on my terms. I will teach the class as I always used to…no interference. Can you promise me that?"

"Oh, yes! It will be for only one day, so it can't matter if you don't adhere completely with the core directives. Does that mean you really will come?"

"Yes. I'll be there by seven o'clock. Is the class still held in the modular unit at the back of the campus?"

"Yes. I'll have the enrollment list and lesson book waiting for you when you sign in at the office. You are a life saver! Thank you, so much."

Tillie put down her phone with mixed emotions. She'd missed the classroom, so she felt a thrill of anticipation, but along with it came just a pinch of anxiety. What if she'd lost her touch?

Agatha's hungry yowl pulled her out of her worries.

"No point in fretting, is there, Aggie. The time for second thoughts was before I accepted the assignment, right? Let's see what I have in the cupboard to fill that bottomless pit of a stomach of yours, shall we?"

With her misgivings brushed aside, Tillie filled the cat's dish from a pouch of salmon flavored Kitty Num-Nums and began looking ahead to the next day's adventure.

25

Tillie had signed in and was exploring her classroom well before school time the next morning.

Seeing the Stars and Stripes were not on display, she rummaged in the storage cupboard until she found a small American flag on a stick and anchored it to her desk at the front of the room by jamming it into a can of modeling clay from the same cupboard.

She sat at the teacher's desk reviewing the lesson plan and teacher's notes. Shaking her head and emitted a soft, "Tsk, tsk!" she began lining things out and scratching her own comments in the margins.

As class time neared, a cluster of preteen boys began to gather outside the door, pushing, shoving and swearing at each other. A rough-looking older boy poked his head into the room and, seeing Tillie at the desk, turned to his younger companions with a mocking laugh, saying, "You won't believe who's subbing for Hanson today; it's old Mrs. Santa Claus. Wanna bet I can get her to cry before lunch?"

When the first bell rang, students began to shuffle into the room, milling about, pointing at Tillie, and whispering.

The second bell sounded, but only one or two of the fifteen children took any notice or sat down.

"Class, please take a seat and come to order," Tillie said, standing as tall as possible at the front of the room and looking each student in the eye until all were seated.

"My name is Mrs. Thistlethwaite and I am your teacher for today. I have written my name on the board for you, but you may address me as Mrs. T., if you find my full name too difficult to pronounce."

There were whispers and titters which Tillie ignored as she did a head count of the students.

Knowing students often liked to prank substitutes during the attendance roll call, she had developed the habit of counting heads. If the total matched the attendance list, she simply marked everyone present, as they were on this day. She marked the attendance in the teacher's attendance software on the computer and was ready to begin the day.

"As your substitute teacher, I am your guest in this class today and I expect to be treated with the same good manners you would give to a guest in your home," she said. "I won't bother trying to match your name to your assigned seats, as I assume today you are sitting in seats you prefer, instead of those you were assigned by Mr. Hanson. When I call upon you during this class please stand and give me your name before responding. Is that understood? Giving your correct name will enable me to award any points earned correctly. Demerits will be recorded based upon a photograph, so Mr. Hanson can discipline the appropriate party upon his return."

Saying this, she picked up her phone and took a picture of the class, many of whom were sitting open-mouthed.

"Please stand for the Pledge of Allegiance to the flag," she said, gesturing to the flag on her desk.

The students looked at each other in confusion and a girl in the back said, "We don't do that."

"Yeah, that's racist!" someone else called out.

"I usually like to start the day with the Pledge, but today I see we need to have a lesson..," she said, and a few children looked smug at having thwarted her plans, until she continued, "...*first* and then the Pledge."

Leaning against her desk she pointed to the older boy she'd seen peek in before the bell rang.

"Please stand and state your name."

The boy seemed about to resist, but when Tillie smiled, took one step toward him, and snapped his picture, he slid out of his seat.

"Rico," he mumbled.

"Speak up, Rico, please, and tell me why you think saying the Pledge of Allegiance is, as you said, racist."

"Because not everyone comes from here, you know," he said.

"You mean because some people in the class were not born in this country, is that right?"

"Yeah."

"Is that how the rest of you understand it? Is saying a Pledge of Allegiance to this country racist because some people were born in another country? Those who agree, please raise your hand."

After looking at each other, a few hands went up and eventually all were raised.

"Good. It's unanimous. We have a general misconception we can clear up quite easily. You each have a tablet computer on your desk. Please look up the definition of the word 'racism.' We must be sure we all know exactly what makes an action racist."

The students opened their search engines, racing to be the first to announce the definition.

They soon began to shout out the definitions and Tillie called on them to read what they'd found. She wrote on the blackboard: *racism is a belief that race is the primary determinant of human traits and capacities and that racial differences produce an inherent superiority of a particular race.*

"Do you agree that what I've written is an accurate meaning, based on all the dictionaries you researched?" she asked and the students nodded. "Good."

"Now, you all agreed the Pledge of Allegiance is racist, but I can't see how that definition applies. Can you?"

There was a general squirming and shuffling and eventually one hand went up.

"Please stand and state your name."

"Ramona Hess," a skinny blond girl said, standing beside her desk.

"Can you answer the question, Ramona?"

"It's racist because it says that America is the superior race to all the others."

"Well, now, just where in the Pledge do we find that claim?" Tillie asked.

As she suspected, none of these children had ever learned to recite the Pledge of Allegiance, so Tillie proceeded to write it on the board. Once it was written, she asked the class to read it aloud with her. In their curiosity the children had forgotten to resist the new substitute and were eager to prove her wrong.

"Which of these sentences indicates a racial superiority?" she asked.

Rico stood up.

"Yes, Rico?"

"It doesn't say it in so many words, but it just sounds like we are supposed to think there's something special about America. Like we are better than other countries."

"So, can we agree the Pledge is not overtly racist?" she asked. After explaining the word "overt" the students nodded. "But, you object because it *implies* this country is better than others and some of you are, or might be, from a different country, is that right?

"If you were born in another country, please stand," she said, and two students stood. "If your parents were born in another country, please stand, also."

Three more students stood.

"Very good. You may be seated. So, because you or your parents were originally from another country, you do not want to pledge allegiance to this flag?"

Getting a few nods, she asked, "Are you or your parents staying in this country against your will? No, well, I'm glad to know you aren't prisoners. Did someone force you to come here? No. So then, you and your parents must prefer this country to the one you left, right? One might even suppose a person only comes to the USA because they think it is superior to their old country."

Tillie was pleased to see some of the students were wrestling with unfamiliar ideas.

A dark-skinned girl in the back of the room stood.

"My name's Dashah Washington. My mom says the flag is all about white privilege and we shouldn't be *indocrinated* by saying a pledge to it."

"That's an interesting point, Dashah. Saying and memorizing The Pledge of Allegiance to the flag of our country might seem like indoctrination to some people, while others think it encourages patriotism. I think we need to define a couple of more terms. Please look up the meaning of 'pledge' and 'allegiance'.

The rest of the morning was spent in discovery of the concepts of patriotism, symbolism, and an in depth discussion of the phrase, "Liberty and Justice for all."

Before breaking for lunch, Tillie led the now compliant class in reciting the pledge.

When the bell rang, a cluster of students gathered around Tillie's desk.

"What are we going to learn after lunch, Mrs. T.?" Rico asked.

Tillie pulled an artifact, an ancient Incan clay bowl, from her tote bag, unwrapped it and held it up.

"This bowl was made by someone just like you who lived in South America hundreds of years ago. I dug it up from the site of his village on an archaeological expedition. I thought you might like to hear about what life was like in that country long ago, and perhaps learn to make a bowl like this, too, if we have time."

The chattering children ran off to the cafeteria and Tillie pulled her lunch box from her tote and ate at her desk, tired, but satisfied with her morning's session.

*

Tillie's substitute teaching had forced a postponement of their planned surveillance, leaving Slim free for the morning.

He felt like he needed to alone for messing up their stakeout the day before, so he decided to tail Whipple on his own, without telling Tillie of his plans.

While Tillie was getting acquainted with her class, Slim prepared for his solo investigation. After a quick breakfast, he drove to the usual spot and waited.

Just as on the previous days, Danny left home with a full backpack and headed toward the park.

Slim drove ahead, got out, and laid in wait for Whipple out of sight in a spot further along the park trail, assuming he would take the same route as before.

As predicted, Whipple soon appeared on the path and Slim managed to follow the younger man undetected for about one hundred yards before stepping on a dried twig and breaking it with a loud snap.

Danny whirled around in time to see Slim duck behind a tree.

"You, again!" he cried out. "What do you want, old man?"

Slim stepped into view, trying desperately to think of a cover story, but his mind had gone blank.

Danny shouted, "Get away from me!" and picked up a large rock from beside the path. He held it threateningly and then shocked Slim by hurling it toward him.

Slim turned away, but the rock hit him in the side of the head, knocking him to the ground.

Danny, looking surprised at the success of his throw, cautiously approached Slim and nudged him with his foot.

"Hey, get up," he said.

When Slim didn't respond, Danny looked over his shoulder to see if he was being observed, and then dragged the unconscious man out of sight into the weeds before jogging back to the path and hurrying down the trail.

*

Waiting for her ride after school, Tillie called Slim from the nearest bus stop. She was eager to tell him all about her day and to arrange for their next stakeout, but her call went straight to voice mail.

"Oh, that man," she said, rolling her eyes.

She supposed he must have let the battery run down again.

No worries, though. He was due to join her for dinner that evening.

The bus pulled up, she found a seat and began to make plans for their next surveillance.

Her successful day of teaching had restored Tillie's confidence in her gut instincts. She didn't know if Danny Whipple was responsible for Honora's disappearance, but she was convinced he was up to no good and she was determined to find out exactly what it was.

26

The trapdoor thumped closed when her captor left, leaving Honora alone once again.

She listened for any sounds of the man's return and when all remained quiet, she lifted her blindfold and began pushing at the chain around her waist.

She'd been fed only about once a day in her confinement and, even with her restricted movement, wasn't consuming enough calories to maintain her weight. Gnawing hunger was her frequent companion and her normally slim figure was growing leaner with each day.

Since noticing that the chain slipped around her waist and was no longer constricting, she'd been trying to eat even less.

When the man noticed she was leaving food on her plate, Honora told him she had no appetite now that she couldn't dance and he hadn't tried to force her to eat.

Yesterday she'd almost managed to push the chain over her prominent hip bones.

She hoped today was the day when she would finally be free of the heavy links.

Honora pushed the chain down over one hip and it dug into her flesh above the other. After wiggling it back and forth, over and over, biting her lip against the pain, the chain finally clattered to the floor around her feet.

"What now?" she said aloud, stepping out of the loop of metal.

Honora was stunned by her success. Never daring to believe she could get free of the hated chain, she hadn't formulated a plan.

She shuffled across the room, trying to remember the layout from what she'd seen the time the hatch was opened before she pulled down her blindfold.

Bumping into the table, she felt for the

lantern she'd seen then, but her groping fingers failed to find it. She turned toward the wall and felt along each of the metal shelves, scraping her fingers on the sharp edges, but not finding the lantern.

When she came to the end of the shelving, she felt over the floor with her feet, encountering her toilet bucket, the plastic chair, and a stack of magazines, but no lantern.

Had he taken the lantern away with him?

When she knocked into the ladder, she scrambled up, slipping briefly in her haste, until her head touched the trapdoor. She pushed with both hands as hard as she could. She almost fell off the ladder, but the door didn't budge. Feeling for a latch or handle, her fingers encountered only a rough, concrete surface.

With a whimper, she climbed back down, discouraged.

Honora slumped onto her cot and gave in to hot tears of frustration before screaming out for help.

Exhausted, and with a raw, sore throat, she tried to pull herself together. She needed to use her wits, if she were ever going to get free.

Getting to her feet and methodically making her way around her prison, she felt for anything she could use to make her escape.

Back at the shelving unit, her fingers closed around a small piece of cardboard. She felt all its surfaces and recognized it as a book of matches, giving her a spark of hope. If she could locate the lantern, she would have a way to light it.

The matchbook felt almost full, with a double row of matches, so she dared to strike one. The first broke without igniting, but she held the second closer to the match head when striking and it flared to life, briefly illuminating the cell.

She scanned the room, but the flickering light did not reveal a lantern.

There was an empty coffee can on one shelf and she snatched it up, placing it in the center of the table before the match burned down to her fingers.

Not wanting to waste any precious matches, she groped in the dark to the pile of magazines and grabbed one. Tearing off a page, she twisted it into a taper, stuck it into the can, and lit a match, setting the paper on fire. It flared up, but quickly turned to crumbling ash.

Honora tried tearing and rolling more pages together in a bundle and soon had a longer lasting light.

Having her vision restored, after so many days of darkness was intoxicating. She wanted to luxuriate in the sensation, but she had to keep her mind on escape.

If her attacker kept to his schedule, she had until at least the next day to come up with a way to get out, but there was no guarantee. He'd sometimes visited several times on a single day, sitting beside her, stroking her hair, and talking wildly about their future together.

She thought he was toying with her,

enjoying his control over her and her fear, while savoring the anticipation of whatever his ultimate plan might be. These were the most terrifying moments of her captivity. She fought to keep her mind blank and not let it fill with all the unspeakable possibilities.

*

"This is great!" John Ransom said, putting down the phone and signaling for Sergeant Forester to come into his office.

"What's up?" Forester asked.

"That was my contact with the Medford police. The FBI has arrested the suspected Coastal Killer. They found evidence, in his apartment and in his truck, tying him to both the girl who survived and the Oceanside victim. So far, nothing connecting him to our girl, but they have high hopes the perp will tell them where she is, and confess to all his other victims, in order to avoid the death penalty. Oh, man, it feels good to know this guy is off the streets, at last. As soon as I clear it with the boss, I'll hop on a plane for LA."

"Before you go, we should eat the last of Mrs. T.'s cinnamon rolls to celebrate," Forester said. "I'll get the coffee."

"Are you sure? I thought your wife wanted you to trim your middle," Ransom said, looking pointedly at the slight bulge rolling over Forester's belt.

"I can return to my diet with gusto after we get these temptations out of the way," Forester said, grinning.

27

Rumpled and out of sorts from hours waiting for his flight in Portland, the hassle at security, and his cramped seat on the plane squeezed in beside an obnoxious, over-sized insurance salesman, John Ransom exited LAX and flagged down a cab to take him to the FBI building.

Whizzing through frantic Los Angeles traffic, he fought an urge to ask the cabdriver to slow down and tried to think about the interview ahead. Portland traffic could be pretty nasty, but these California drivers were insane.

Ransom allowed himself a brief moment of longing for the quiet highways and byways around Tillamook, and then pulled his notepad from his jacket pocket to refresh his mind with the name of his FBI contact, Special Agent Harmony Billings.

Once at his destination, Ransom entered the

building and walked toward the reception desk.

"Detective Ransom?" an attractive, smartly dressed woman in her mid-thirties approached with her hand outstretched.

"That's right. How could you tell?" he replied, shaking her hand.

"Your carry-on bag and general air of fatigue were a dead giveaway. I didn't get to be an FBI Special Agent for nothing," she said with a smile. "I'm Harmony Billings. I'm glad you could make it on such short notice, although I'm afraid we won't be interviewing the suspect together, after all. He's lawyered up. However, I can let you see what we have so far and you can bring me up to speed on your missing person."

Agent Billings walked Ransom to the elevator as she spoke and they rode up to her office.

"I'm disappointed not to be able to ask this guy some questions," Ransom said, sliding into the visitor's chair and pulling a file folder from his shoulder bag and handing it across the desk.

"I have a feeling once his lawyer sees the evidence we have, he will be in the mood to make a deal. That's our best shot at getting information on your victim," she said, opening the file and starting to review the contents.

After reading the reports and discussing the Anniston case, Harmony took John downstairs to have a look at the man in custody.

Viewing the suspect through a reinforced window in the holding cell door, Ransom felt revulsion and rage as he recalled the things this man had done.

For the first time, he hoped he was wrong about Honora Anniston being another of the man's victims. He wanted the case solved, but not with such a resolution.

Harmony escorted Ransom down to the lobby.

"It's almost one o'clock," John said. "Have you had lunch? I'd like to thank you for all your help."

Impulsively and totally out of character, Harmony surprised herself by agreeing to take her lunch break with Ransom.

"There's a good Mexican place just around the corner. Well, to be fair, there's a good Mexican restaurant or tortillaria around just about every corner in LA. Do you like Mexican food?" she asked.

"My favorite. Lead the way."

*

Back at the office later that afternoon, Harmony worked on a stack of reports, trying to get caught up on the backlog which had accumulated during the Coastal Killer investigation. As lead agent, she had the most paperwork to complete, but she would also get the lion's share of credit for the arrest. All in all, it was a fair trade.

From time to time while reducing the events of the investigation into dry procedures for the report forms, her thoughts strayed to her meeting with the Oregon detective. She'd enjoyed the brief time they'd spent together. John Ransom seemed like a good guy. It was just her luck he lived almost a thousand miles away.

Her parents had warned her she might be sacrificing her personal life for a career in crime prevention with the FBI. Harmony had laughed, assuming she would be able to have it all... a successful career, marriage, and family. Now in her mid-thirties, she was beginning to have doubts.

The men she met at work were either career-driven agents or criminals. It was hardly a good dating pool. As an attractive woman, she'd had plenty of opportunities to date agents, but found out they were only interested in convenient hook-ups and not long-term relationships. She would never seriously consider getting involved with a criminal, although she'd learned of other women in law enforcement who had gotten entangled in that sort of dead-end relationship.

On her mother's advice, Harmony had

joined a Christian singles group at her church, but her work schedule kept her from attending either worship or the group meetings on a regular basis. Also, her profession seemed off-putting to many of the civilian men she met.

Ransom took her career in stride, seeming neither overly impressed or resentful of her position. He understood the demands of law enforcement, too.

She was pretty sure he had been thinking of her as a woman, not an FBI agent, when he'd asked her to have lunch with him. However, a thousand miles was too much of an obstacle to overcome, even if he were interested.

Still, it gave Harmony hope there might be someone out there for her, and maybe someone in a bit closer proximity.

28

Slim rolled over with a groan. Opening his swollen eyes, he was confused to find himself outdoors, lying in a weedy gully.

Dizzy and with a throbbing headache, he pushed himself up onto his knees and reached for his phone, patting his pockets before having a vague recollection of leaving it on the charger in his car.

Chilled from the damp ground and aching all over, he bit back nausea and crawled over to a large tree where he pulled himself to his feet.

Slim clung to the tree as a wave of vertigo swept over him. When the earth stopped tilting, he looked around and saw two blurry figures on the nearby path.

He waved to get their attention.

"Are you alright?" a woman asked.

Slim focused hard and the two figures merged into one as his double-vision cleared.

"I seem to have fallen and bumped my head, ma'am. I'm a little dizzy," Slim said.

The jogger, a stocky woman in her forties, walked over to Slim and helped him to keep his balance while he shuffled onto the path with his arm around her shoulders.

"Do you want me to call someone?" she asked. "Your family or an ambulance?"

"No, no. I'm okay. If you wouldn't mind letting me lean on you while I get back to my car, I'm sure I'll be fine once I rest a bit."

Looking doubtful, the woman helped to steady Slim until they reached his car.

"Are you sure, you're okay?" she asked when Slim slid into the driver's seat. "Will you be safe to drive?"

"I'm feeling much better, already. Thanks for your help."

"Well, then, I think you should drive

yourself straight to the ER. That bloody wound on your head needs to be cleaned and checked out."

Slim pulled down the sun visor and looked in the mirror. His eyes widened at a deep, ugly gash on his head and smears of dried blood on his bruised and swollen face. He must have fallen hard. He wished he could remember what he'd been doing in the park all alone and what made him fall.

"I believe I'll do that very thing, ma'am. Thanks so much," he said.

The woman walked back to the jogging trail, turning back with a worried look as Slim started his car and drove slowly away.

Slim wore a similar concerned expression as he steered through the streets with shaking hands. His lack of memory frightened him. Had he fallen from a stroke or a seizure? At his age, losing his mental faculties meant the end of independence and life as he liked to live it.

Maneuvering the car with an extra measure of caution, he managed to arrive safely at the local hospital.

He parked the car, slipped his phone into his pocket and limped into the emergency room. Seeing his bloody head and noting his age, the receptionist immediately called a nurse to take Slim into an exam room.

A doctor examined him and cleaned up the wound on Slim's head, which required several stitches, then admitted him for observation.

"Did I have a stroke, doctor?" Slim asked as he was being admitted.

"I didn't find any signs of one, but we will run a few more tests to see if anything turns up. Right now, I'd say you probably just tripped and hit your head."

"Then, why can't I remember what happened?" Slim asked. "Now, I do recall driving to the park, but after that, nothing until waking up on the ground. And I still don't know why I went there."

"You've got a mild concussion. Brief loss of

memory is common. You may never remember the accident, but everything else should eventually come back to you. You are in remarkable condition for a man of your age," the doctor reassured Slim.

"If you want to keep active, you've got to be active. Anyway that's what my friend, Tillie, always says," Slim replied.

"That's good advice," the doctor said, and then left the exam room.

*

Slim was dozing in a private hospital room when he heard the muffled ringing of his phone from inside the clothes cupboard.

He buzzed for the nurse and asked her to bring it to him.

Still a bit woozy from pain medication and the trauma of his fall, he squinted at the display, noting several missed calls, all from Tillie.

He tapped in her number, leaned back against the pillow, and waited for her to answer.

"Sylvester Michael Bottoms! Where have

you been?" Tillie snapped without preamble, seeing his name on the caller ID.

Slim grinned, recognizing the concern in her voice. When a woman used his full Christian name, he knew he was in trouble.

"It seems I've been taking a little nap in the park for most of the day, today. I don't think I'll be able to make it for dinner tonight," he said.

"Sleeping in the park? What are you talking about? Where are you?" Tillie asked.

"Don't worry. I'm safe and reasonably sound. Not necessarily in my right mind, maybe, but then, when was I ever? I'm all tucked up in a nice, comfy hospital bed, though. Not too much the worse for wear."

"Oh, Slim! What happened?" she asked. "I'm coming right over. Wait there!"

She ended the call without waiting for a response and Slim chuckled as he set the phone on the table beside his bed.

"That Tillie. She is a caution," he mumbled,

closing his eyes.

When Slim next awoke, he saw Tillie sitting beside his bed, reading.

"How long you been here?" he asked, his voice raspy.

"Not long enough. I never should have let you out of my sight," she scolded. "What were you doing in the park all by yourself, anyway?"

"I don't rightly remember, but the doctor says that's normal with a concussion."

Tillie patted his hand and smiled.

"I spoke with the nurse. She says you are going to be just fine. In fact, you might go home tomorrow."

"I'd like that. Right now, I'm just as happy to stay here, though. That fall knocked the stuffings out of me, I guess."

"Don't start feeling sorry for yourself," Tillie said. "You can wallow in bed being pampered tonight, but tomorrow it's up and out of here before you get used to it."

"Yes, dear," Slim said. "Whatever you say."

Tillie stayed with Slim while he ate his dinner, then caught the bus back home.

She fretted while getting ready for bed. An injury like his could spell trouble for someone Slim's age, and beyond that, she couldn't shake the feeling Danny Whipple was involved, somehow.

The doctor had assured her Slim's fall wasn't from a stroke or other underlying condition and she knew Slim was stronger and steadier on his feet than most men his age. He wouldn't simply lose his balance and keel over. And it happened at the park, too. She had a suspicion Slim had been investigating on his own when he'd been hurt.

As she turned off her bedside lamp, Tillie decided to go back to the park the next day and see what she could find out.

*

After a few early morning errands, Tillie was walking from the bus stop when two boys on skateboards whizzed past, one on each side, and her purse was knocked from her hand.

One of the boys stooped down, grabbed the purse, and pushed off, but his companion, looking back, called, "Wait, Jaxon! It's Mrs. T."

The taller of the two boys hopped off his board and walked over to Tillie.

"Well, hello, Rico!" Tillie said. "How nice to see you, again. You went by so fast, I didn't recognize you boys."

"Yeah, uh, sorry we bumped you," Rico said. "Here, Jax picked up your bag for you."

The younger boy skated up and handed Tillie the bag without making eye contact.

"Thank you, Jaxon," she said, taking the handbag. "What brings you boys to my side of town?"

"Just hangin' around," Rico said with a shrug.

"Well, since you aren't too busy, why don't you boys come in for a snack. This is my house here and I've got homemade cookies that need to be eaten," she said, opening her gate.

"My mom says I can't go into people's houses," Jaxon said.

"Is she afraid her precious baby might get took like that dancer girl?" Rico teased.

"Jaxon's mother is simply being cautious, and quite rightly, but she wouldn't mind if you sit on my veranda for cookies and milk, would she?"

"What's a veranda?" Jaxon asked.

"It's a porch, stupid. Come on," Rico said, leading the way.

Tillie soon came out carrying a tray laden with a plate of oatmeal raisin cookies and two tumblers of milk, plus a cup of tea for herself.

"Here we are," she said, joining the boys at the table. "Help yourselves, don't be shy."

The boys each grabbed a cookie and began to eat.

Jaxon looked at Tillie's front garden as he chewed. After he swallowed and was reaching for another cookie he asked, "Why do you got all those dwarfs?"

Tillie looked fondly at the comical characters tucked amongst the greenery.

"Those are garden gnomes. Their cheerful faces keep my flowers happy. They are good luck, too. Just looking at them always makes me smile."

"You're a funny old lady," Jaxon said.

"Shut up, you dope!" Rico said, punching his friend in the arm

"Oh, that's all right. Jaxon is correct. I am an old lady, and a bit funny, too. I'd so much rather be a funny old lady than a grouchy one."

"Are you going to come back and teach us?" Jaxon asked. "Mr. Hanson is a grouch, for sure."

"Don't you boys like Mr. Hanson?"

"Nah, he never smiles and he's always yelling at us. You never yelled," Jaxon said.

"Well, I don't know Mr. Hanson, but I know that when I don't feel liked, it makes me unhappy, so I don't smile. Do you think Mr. Hanson knows you don't like him?"

"He ought to," Rico laughed.

"So, is it any wonder he doesn't seem happy?" she asked. "Stop and think how you would feel if you were the one teaching your class and the students acted as you boys do."

"But, he's the teacher. He doesn't care what we think," Rico said.

"Every teacher is just a person and has the same feelings as you. Being grown up doesn't make us immune to hurt feelings, not even teachers. You try being nicer to your teachers and you just might find they will be nicer to you. I know you can do it, because you were lovely to me."

The two boys sat quietly munching cookies, then drank their milk. Rico stood and prodded Jaxon to get up.

"We gotta go, now. Thanks for the snack," he said, heading toward the steps.

"Before you go, just a word of caution. When riding skateboards, if you see someone walking ahead of you, please pick up your board and walk around. That way you won't *accidentally* knock someone's bag out of their hands."

The boys exchanged guilty looks, trotted out to the sidewalk, and skated off with a wave.

Tillie chuckled and, shaking her head, hurried inside to change for her investigations at the park.

29

Tears of frustration stung Honora eyes. She'd failed to find anything in the cramped space to pry open the trapdoor. She'd even tried to loosen one of the pipes on the wall to use as a lever, but with her bare hands it was impossible.

Her only hope of escape was to flee up the ladder when the hatch was already open. That meant somehow overpowering the man on his next visit. She was sure she was smaller than her captor and she would need a weapon and the element of surprise if she had any chance of success, especially in her weakened condition.

The underground room was sparsely furnished and her hectic searches turned up nothing she could use against her captor.

Honora had considered the heavy chain she'd wriggled out of, now lying on the floor.

Swung with force, it could incapacitate a man, but when she'd tried to detach it from the pipe by her bed, the padlock held fast.

In the flickering light of her last taper, her gaze fell upon the latrine bucket, giving her an idea.

Gathering her radio, the jars, and other heavy items from the shelves, plus the stack of magazines, she dumped them into the empty bucket, and lifted it to test its weight.

If she was able to catch the man off guard, swing it hard, and connect with his head, she just might have enough time to get up the ladder and slam the hatch before he recovered.

She pictured this desperate act of violence and felt a surge of fear. Could she do it? She'd never harmed another person. What would the man do to her if she failed?

Honora was briefly paralyzed with indecision until her Bible verse about courage came into her mind and restored her resolve. It would be risky, but it was her only chance.

As she made up her mind, the flame in the can burned out.

In the familiar darkness, she wrapped her blindfold around the bucket's handle for a better grip, and sat on the cot to wait.

She prayed for strength as her muscles trembled, her stomach churned, and the minutes dragged past.

*

After the young ex-purse snatchers left, Tillie changed into her sleuthing clothes and caught a bus to the park.

She walked the path slowly, trying to see anything which might tell her where, and more importantly, why, Slim had fallen.

Coming to a spot well beyond where they'd lain in wait for Danny, she saw what looked like drag marks in the soft turf.

Two furrows led off the path into the tall weeds toward a spot where the grass was matted down into a depression almost as long as Slim's lanky form.

Slim must have fallen on the path and been dragged into the brush. But, who would do that? And why? Slim said he hadn't been robbed.

Tillie could almost imagine Danny seeing Slim fall and simply walking off and leaving. But why drag the unconscious man into the weeds?

Had Danny thought Slim was dead? He would only want to hide the body if he were responsible. She couldn't believe the boy was capable of such a violent act.

Tillie was still standing off in the brush trying to make sense of her suspicions when she heard footsteps approaching on the path.

She ducked down out of sight and was not surprised to see Danny stroll past, his backpack bulging.

Tillie crept after him as quietly as possible, staying low and out of sight. When she saw him leave the trail and walk into the woods, she was afraid he'd noticed her and was circling around to grab her.

With a pounding heart, she considered turning back until she glimpsed him walking away through the trees.

"Faint heart ne'er won anything for an old lady, that's my motto," she whispered.

Following at what she hoped was a safe distance, she lost sight of him in the thicket. When she emerged from the grove of trees onto a meadow, Danny was nowhere to be seen.

She knew this clearing was the abandoned site of an industrial development begun decades earlier, but halted by environmentalists before its completion. A few slabs of concrete, rusted pipes, and what looked like maintenance bunkers overgrown with native plants dotted the field.

Where could Danny have gone? Tillie was sure she would have seen him if he'd doubled back through the woods.

She was wandering around trying to decide what to do, when she heard a frightened scream and a shout. She whirled around just in time to see a blond head emerge from a clump of weeds and immediately disappear.

*

When Honora heard the hatch being moved, she'd jumped up, grabbing the weighted bucket in both hands, and stood beside the ladder; her stomach twisting and her adrenaline-primed muscles aching for action.

Blinking in the sudden stream of sunshine, she lifted the bucket to shoulder height and twisted her body in preparation.

Danny's feet appeared on the ladder and she wanted to smash them with the bucket, but she held back. This would only work if she could hit him on the head.

When his feet hit the floor, he saw the empty cot and swiveled around just as Honora swung the bucket with all her strength, hitting him in the side of the head.

He crumpled to the floor and she leapt over

his body onto the ladder, her feet slipping in her panicked scramble.

Her head cleared the hatch, but before she could climb out, Danny, with blood running down his face, grabbed her feet and pulled. Honora kicked, lost her balance, and fell to the floor, stunned and remained unmoving, crumpled in an awkward position.

Danny clamored up the ladder to close the hatch. He poked his head up to see if anyone had heard Honora's scream and saw a surprised Tillie looking back at him from about twenty yards away.

He looked down at Honora, who hadn't moved, trying to decide what to do.

"Danny?" Tillie called. "Danny Whipple, is that you?"

Danny climbed up and stood beside the hatch.

"Go away," he shouted. "This is my private place. You got no business here. Leave me alone."

"Is this your private little hideaway,

Danny?" Tillie asked, backing away slowly. "How nice. Well, I won't bother you, now. Tell your mother I said hello."

Seeing Tillie's uncase, and afraid she had seen Honora, he ran over and grabbed the old woman roughly.

"You're not going to tell my mother anything. Come on!" he said, manhandling Tillie and forcing her down the ladder.

She stumbled against Honora, who was just coming around. Seeing the girl was injured, Tillie crouched down beside her.

"What have you done to this poor girl?" she cried.

"Get up! Both of you!" Danny barked, nudging them over toward the pallet with his foot.

"Honora dear, are you all right?" Tillie asked, putting her arms around the shaking girl.

Honora sniffed and nodded, wincing in pain.

"Shut up!" Danny screamed.

He paced around the small space, wringing his hands together and muttering under his breath. Seeing the overturned bucket, he bent down and picked up the radio.

"I gave you this for being good! Now you are not good and you can't have it. You broke it, too. It's got a big crack."

He slumped dejectedly into the chair, turning the radio over in his hands.

Tillie was stunned. She'd suspected Danny was up to something, but never believed he was holding this poor girl captive. She realized he was seriously mentally deranged.

Someone had to get help and Tillie thought the boy's distraction with the radio might be her chance. When she made a move toward the ladder, he jumped up, throwing the radio aside.

"No, you don't!" he said, pushing her back down beside Honora.

Danny pulled the rucksack off Tillie's back and threw it across the room before removing the scarf from her pith helmet and using it to tie her hands behind her back.

Honora slumped over on the cot without Tillie's support and remained still.

Tillie feared the girl was seriously injured in her fall from the ladder.

"Sit up!" Danny said, shaking Honora's shoulder, but although her eyes opened, they remained unfocused.

He hadn't brought the key to the padlock, so he grabbed the clothesline he'd used when he'd first abducted her and tied her limp hands together with it.

Honora seemed so out of it that she didn't seem capable of walking, so he didn't bother binding her legs or tying her to the pipe. The old woman could scarcely climb down the ladder, so he was sure she couldn't climb up it to escape.

Satisfied his captives were secure, Danny picked up his backpack and stepped onto the ladder.

"I was bringing you good food and a treat, too, but you won't get anything, now. Maybe I will come back and maybe I won't. So there!" he shouted, spraying spittle from his lips.

He climbed out of the bunker and slammed down the hatch cover, plunging the underground room into darkness.

"Oh dear," Tillie sighed. "I had to prove my theory, didn't I? Pride goes before a fall, I always say."

30

"How'd it go with the FBI yesterday," Sergeant Forester asked as Detective Ransom walked through the office.

"The perp lawyered up before I got there, so I didn't get an interview with him."

"Was it a wasted trip, then?"

"Not really. I met the lead agent on the case and she let me get a look at the creep and read the files," Ransom said.

"She?" Forester asked, raising his eyebrows. "Was she a real hard case?"

"Not really. She was helpful. She promised to keep in touch and to let us know if they manage to connect this suspect with the Anniston disappearance."

Ransom walked into his own office, put his briefcase on the desk, and pulled out the copies of the files Harmony had given him.

He picked up her business card and rubbed it between his fingers, thinking about their casual lunch together.

He gave himself a mental shake, stuffed the card into his desk drawer, grabbed his mug, and headed to the break room for coffee. Time to get to work.

*

Tillie failed to turn up at the hospital by the time of his release, so Slim called her. When she didn't answer, he left a message to say he was driving himself home and hoped to see her later. He'd expected her to show up at his bedside, bright and early, but he knew she was a busy lady and probably had things to attend to.

When she didn't answer any of his subsequent calls and hadn't come to see him by late afternoon, he began to worry. He was still too shaky to go out looking for her, but he made calls to a few of her friends and learned none of them had heard from her that day.

Where could she be? It was not like her, at all, to ignore a friend who'd just come home from the hospital.

Now, he was afraid it was Tillie who was missing.

*

Danny Whipple was restless. He couldn't think what to do.

At home, in his bedroom, he whittled on a piece of wood while muttering about how the old woman had spoiled things with Honora.

In his mind, Honora's escape attempt had been instigated, somehow, by Tillie. He'd convinced himself Honora would never have tried to hurt him, unless she had been provoked. Honora liked him, even loved him, although she didn't know it, yet. They were going to be married one day; that was part of his plan.

As he fretted, the wood in his hand began to take on the form of a garden gnome with an uncanny resemblance to Tillie Thistlethwaite.

While the carving took shape in his hands, an idea formed in his twisted mind.

*

With no word from Tillie by dinnertime, Slim was seriously concerned and called her friend, Detective Ransom.

"That's right, detective. No one's seen or heard from her since she visited me in the hospital last night. I'd go looking for her, myself, but I'm still not too steady on my pins," Slim said.

"I'm sure she's fine, Mr. Bottoms. We both know what Mrs. T. is like. She probably took it into her head to fly off on safari, or something," Ransom joked.

"She wouldn't go off anywhere without telling anyone, not when she knew I might get out of the hospital this morning," Slim insisted.

"Okay. I don't think you have anything to worry about, but if it will make you feel better, I'll make a welfare check on her, right away. I've got your number, so I'll call you back to let you know she's safe and sound."

Ransom clicked off his phone looking worried.

He'd meant it when he reassured Bottoms, but he had to admit it was unusual for Mrs. T. to go off without letting anyone know where she would be.

He grabbed his jacket off the back of his chair and went out.

31

Honora didn't move while Tillie worked at untying the knotted scarf around her own wrists.

"Is the poor girl semi-comatose or merely sunk in depression at her failed escape?" Tillie wondered as she worked.

Luckily, Danny was unfamiliar with the stretchy properties of a chiffon scarf and in a short time Tillie had her hands free. She immediately set to work on the rope knots holding Honora.

"We'll soon have you out of this," Tillie said.

Honora simply moaned in response.

"Are you badly hurt, dear?" Tillie asked, feeling renewed anger at the Whipple boy.

Her ire was increased by frustration as she struggled with the knots in the rope holding Honora's wrists.

Fuming at the boy's rough treatment, Tillie

remembered the rucksack containing her detecting tools which Danny had tossed across the room. There might be something in the bag she could use on the stubborn rope.

It was difficult getting her bearings in the inky darkness, but Tillie shuffled across the floor holding her hands out in front of her until she touched the far wall. From there she edged around the room until her foot nudged the rucksack. Carrying the bag with her as she made her way back to the cot, she bumped her head, hard, on the metal ladder and was momentarily stunned by the impact.

"Too bad seeing stars doesn't brighten up the room, any," she quipped, hoping to cheer Honora. "Now, let's see what we've got here."

Feeling around inside the bag, her fingers recognized a can opener and a pair of tweezers. She pried at the knots with the two implements until she was able to loosen the rope enough to use her fingers.

Honora's hands were soon free, but the girl still didn't move.

"Our hands are untied now, so we'd better waste no time getting ourselves out of this hole before that awful boy returns," Tillie chattered at her unresponsive companion.

"You are a brave girl and you almost made it out of here, but now that the boy's on alert we won't be able to catch him by surprise. All things considered, brute force isn't much of an option, so we'll need to rely on cleverness. A strong mind can overcome strong muscles, I always say."

Tillie pulled Honora upright, keeping up her one-sided conversation, and began rubbing the girl's cold arms, attempting to revive her.

She plopped the pith helmet onto Honora's head and secured it with the scarf, and then pulled a bright orange sweater from her rucksack. She thrust the girl's limp arms into the sleeves and buttoned her up. The over-sized sweater's warmth soon revived her.

Shivering, Honora whispered her thanks and sat up straighter.

"How are we ever getting out of here? He always latches that trapdoor," she said when her trembling subsided.

"Maybe this time he forgot," Tillie suggested. "He left here in quite a snit, after all. Let's just check, shall we?"

Tillie slid her feet in the direction of the ladder and, when she found it, stepped carefully onto each rung. It had been many years since she had climbed a ladder and she wasn't enjoying it.

Finally at the top, she pushed on the hatch as hard as she could. She felt it shift ever so slightly, but despite all her exercises, it was too heavy for Tillie to lift.

"It doesn't seem to be latched, dear. Perhaps if you join me on the ladder, we can push together and get it open."

"I'm dizzy," Honora breathed as she stood up.

"Take your time," Tillie said and soon heard the girl's dragging footsteps.

Honora's foot slipped on a rung and she lost her balance, nearly knocking them both off, before she steadied herself and climbed up behind Tillie.

"Now, just reach up here over my head and when I give the signal, we'll push together and open this silly thing, right?" Tillie said, and felt Honora nod.

"On three, then. One-two-three!"

The heavy metal and concrete slab lifted a few inches, allowing light to seep in. They'd managed to knock it off-center a bit, and when their combined strength failed, it didn't fall completely shut.

The light, although dim, encouraged both women.

"Oh, that was a good first try, dear. I think if we each step up one more rung on the ladder we will have better leverage on our next try."

They maneuvered themselves higher on the

ladder and after a few more tries their joint desperation succeeded in heaving the cover partially aside.

Tillie felt weak from her efforts and her ears were ringing.

"Do you think you can slip through, Honora?" she asked, easing aside to let the girl pass.

"I'd have never made it before he trapped me here, but I've lost weight and I think I can, now," she said, climbing over Tillie.

Tillie's borrowed sweater snagged a bit on the rough concrete, but it protected the girl's skin as she wriggled through the narrow opening. Honora pulled herself out, crouched above the hatch, and leaned back in with her arm outstretched.

"Come on, I'll pull you up," she urged.

"Oh, I'm afraid not, dear. I'd never get through the eye of that needle. I've eaten too much of my own baking. No, you run along and get help.

I'll just wait here."

Honora tried to argue, but she finally accepted Tillie's suggestion and, promising to bring help, she stumbled toward the shelter of the woods.

Her own limbs trembling, Tillie made her way back to the cot.

"Well, Matilda, this is a fine mess you've gotten yourself into," she said and began to pray for Honora while awaiting rescue.

*

The sun was setting when John Ransom parked in front of Tillie's cottage. He felt certain this trip was unnecessary, but being treated to some of her delectable pastries would make the effort worthwhile.

He opened the gate and walked up the path, noticing a new addition to Mrs. T's gnome collection; a miniature lady gnome carved from wood stood beside her front door.

Ransom rang the bell and picked up the

figure while waiting for Mrs. T. to appear. He was surprised to note the woman was portrayed in modern dress instead of a traditional gnomish costume like the rest of Tillie's collection.

A closer inspection revealed the carving's uncanny resemblance to Mrs. T. and gave Ransom a bad feeling. It reminded him of the hand-carved dog figure left before the body of Mrs. Dumont's stolen dog turned up.

He rang the bell, again, and began knocking loudly, but the only response was Agatha's mournful yowl on the other side of the door.

Ransom walked around the cottage peering in the windows, and rattled the knob on the back door.

The house was dark and the door was locked.

Ransom returned to his car, still carrying the carving.

Something was wrong.

When he returned to his office, he opened

the file box holding the dog carving and took both wooden figures to the forensics department.

He asked the technicians to see if they could discover anything tying the two carvings together or giving a clue about who might have carved them.

Now that the FBI had taken over the Coastal Killer case and had the suspect in custody, the missing persons task force was only awaiting proof that Honora was also a victim of this monster before being disbanded. Ransom could concentrate on the animal abuse case and try to see what possible connection there was to Mrs. T.

Back at his desk, he reread her report to the tip line. She'd mentioned something about a carving then, too. It hadn't led to a Coastal Killer connection, but perhaps they had a local artist who was also an animal abuser and she'd somehow run afoul of this person.

He called Officer Willis into his office.

"Yes, sir?"

"Willis, I'd like you to go see our missing girl's dance teacher. She has a carving which may relate to her student's disappearance. Get the carving, give her a receipt, and drop it off with Forensics. Let the teacher know we'll return it, unharmed. Here's the address," Ransom said, handing over a slip of paper.

Willis nodded and went out.

It may be a waste of time, but Ransom wanted to cover all the bases.

With a frown of concentration, he shuffled the case files for a few moments, and then closed the folder, slapped it down on the desk, and stood up, deciding to interview the boy in the report the next day. Although the story was farfetched, it was his only lead to Mrs. T.

He told himself she was probably off feeding the homeless, learning the marimba, or taking a lesson in Swahili, but he couldn't shake a feeling of foreboding.

*

Back in his apartment, Ransom threw his jacket onto the sagging sofa, removed his tie, and put his service pistol into the safe before heading into the kitchen.

He stood staring blankly into the refrigerator before deciding he wasn't really hungry.

He grabbed an apple, a beer, and a chunk of cheese and took them into the living room where he switched on the television for the evening news. Instead of a news anchor, the screen filled with an overly excited game show contestant buying a vowel. Ransom realized he was too late for the newscast and turned the set off.

Munching the apple while half-heartedly scanning the newspaper, he made a decision. He tossed the apple core at the overflowing trash bin and began searching through the pockets of his suit jacket.

He found only crumpled receipts and some

lint and then remembered putting Harmony's card into his desk drawer at the office.

With no idea of what he'd planned to say to her, he thought it was probably just as well he didn't have her card with him. He'd have looked like an idiot calling her with nothing to say. If he'd wanted to get an update on the Coastal Killer case he could do that during office hours the next day.

Of course, it wasn't the case he was interested in, so he had no business calling her, at all. Long-distant relationships never worked.

Deciding to read the biography of Andrew Jackson he'd started earlier in the week, but after seeing Harmony's soft eyes and pretty face rather than the words on the page, he became annoyed with himself.

"Come on!" he muttered, slamming the book shut. "I don't need any more stress in my life."

He pulled his notebook out of his jacket and reviewed his notes on the dog abuse case, looking for possible links to Tillie's disappearance.

32

In her attached garage, Mimsy Waits pushed the empty plastic dishes from her microwaved dinner into the trash and stepped back into her kitchen as her doorbell rang.

She peeked out and saw a policeman on her doorstep.

Running her fingers through her hair and smoothing her blouse, she opened the door with a puzzled expression.

"Good evening, ma'am. Are you Mimsy Waits?"

"Yes. What's the matter, officer?"

"You're the dancing teacher, right?" Willis asked.

"That's right."

"I'm sorry to intrude, but may I come in?"

"Okay," Mimsy stepped back to allow the

officer to enter. "What's this about?"

"I'm Officer Willis, Weldon Willis. I was told you received an unusual carving a few days ago, right after one of your students went missing. Is that right?"

"Yes, it was left at the studio. I don't know who sent it."

"Can I see it?" Willis asked.

"It's in the den. Come this way," she said, leading him into the room and gesturing to the statue.

Willis scanned the collection of dance memorabilia on the shelf with the carving.

"You a ballet dancer, too?" he asked, picking up a framed photo.

"I was. That's me in the second row, on the end," Mimsy pointed. "I was a lot younger then, of course. You probably wouldn't recognize me."

"Pretty," Willis said. "You haven't changed all that much. Why'd you give up dancing?"

"Oh, I was only a professional for a very

short time. The dancing world in New York is pretty competitive. It got hard to pay the bills, so I came home and opened my dance studio."

"New York, huh? I never met a real ballet dance before," Willis said, with a grin. "The guys at the station are gonna be jealous."

Mimsy blushed, not certain if he was serious, or if he was making fun of her.

"You came about the statue. This is it," she picked it up and handed it to Willis.

"Oh, right," he said. "I'll give you a receipt, but I need to take this back to the station. I hope you don't mind."

"If it will help you find Honora, I don't mind at all. In fact, when I first saw it, I thought it might have something to do with her. It looks like her. See?"

"You're right. This thing does resemble the pictures I've seen. Of course, it sort of looks like you, too. I suppose all pretty ballet dancers look alike."

Mimsy looked skeptically at Willis, holding his gaze, until he blushed and looked away. Seeing his reaction, her expression changed to a delighted smile.

"Thanks, Officer Willis," she said. "When will I be able to come and reclaim the carving? I've grown to like it."

"Well, I can bring it back when the lab gets through with it. Why don't you give me your phone number, so I can call and arrange to bring it by?" Willis said, pulling out his notebook. "You can call me Weldon, if you like," he added under his breath.

Mimsy rattled off her mobile number.

"You can reach me at that number, anytime, Weldon," she added, her cheeks getting rosy, again.

"Thanks. Well, um, I'd better go. We'll take real good care of your statue. Thanks."

Mimsy walked Willis to the door, seeing him off with a wave as he climbed into his cruiser.

When he was gone, she walked into the den and picked up the photo, trying to find what Willis had seen. Putting it down, she hugged herself, smiling.

Life had just become several shades brighter for Mimsy.

*

Honora pushed deeply into the shelter of the trees before stopping to catch her breath. Her dance slippers were back in the bunker and the bottoms of her black tights were soon shredded and bloodstained from running over the rough terrain.

Weak from her long confinement and poor nutrition, and fuzzy-headed from her fall, she knew she needed to get help, but she was disoriented in the gathering gloom and had never been in this part of the park's wilderness area.

She stumbled on a root and fell to her hands and knees where she remained, panting. When she heard the rumble of automobile traffic, she pushed to her feet and turned toward the sound and saw headlights flickering through the trees. There would be people in those cars and she could get help.

Feeling hopeful, she staggered through the trees, desperation forcing her forward.

Mistaking her sound of her heart thudding in her ears for approaching footsteps, she panicked, looked back over her shoulder for her pursuer, and ran full-force into a tree. She rebounded back onto the ground with a grunt and was still.

*

In her subterranean prison, Tillie rested in the failing light, wondering if she was soon to reach the end of her long life. She was jerked from her musing when the hatch was jerked fully open and Danny jumped inside.

He looked with shock at the empty ropes on the pallet.

"Where is she?" he yelled, grabbing Tillie by the shoulders and shaking her.

Her teeth rattling, she shouted back.

"Stop that!"

Danny stopped, blinking in surprise.

"Where is she?" he demanded. "What have you done with her?"

"I've done nothing," Tillie replied in her best school-mistress manner. "Now, calm down and be civil, young man."

Whipple frowned and noticed for the first time that Tillie was also unbound.

"You got loose, too, so why are you still here?"

"I waited because I wanted to have a few words with you. Now, you just sit down and explain yourself, Danny Whipple."

Surprisingly, the young man obeyed and pulled over the chair.

"You're not the boss of me," he grumbled, then seeming to realize the truth of what he said, he jumped back up and stood over Tillie menacingly.

"Sit down and show some respect!" Tillie barked. "What would your mother say if she heard you speak to me like that?"

The tactic worked and Danny sat back down.

"What are you gonna tell my mother?" he asked.

"That all depends on you, Danny. You have behaved very badly, you know."

Danny hung his head, saying nothing, while Tillie furiously racked her brain, trying to come up with a strategy to keep herself safe until help arrived. The young man before her, although child-like in many respects, was unpredictable and capable of violence.

"How long have you had this nice secret cave?" she asked him, hoping to keep him distracted. If she could keep him thinking of her as a friend of his mother, rather than a witness to his crime, she might get through the day alive.

"A long time," Danny answered. "It's my place. I can do what I want here and nobody ever tells me I can't."

"What sort of things do you do here? I don't see any of your carving or sculpting supplies."

"I do that at home. Mom likes me to. She thinks I'm a art genius. She's right, too. I can make just about anything from wood or clay."

"I believe that. The dolphin you made for your grandmother was beautiful."

"I made one of you, too," he boasted, then his expression changed as he seemed to recall the reason for this particular carving.

"Oh, really?" Tillie said, going on quickly. "What is your favorite subject to carve? Animals, people, or something else?"

The change of topic seemed to work.

"I like to make boats. Someday I'm going to make a real one and me and Honora will sail away on it," he said with a dreamy expression.

"Boats are nice. I once sailed on a big boat, a ship really, to South America. This was years ago, when my husband was alive."

"You had a husband?" Danny asked in

surprise.

"Oh, yes," Tillie chuckled. "I wasn't always an old lady. My Gerald was an archaeologist. I sometimes accompanied him on his digs. It was fascinating. On this particular trip, we visited a village where the people carved their own boats out of wood, as you do. We rode in one of those hand-carved boats up a big river. I can still remember the way the smooth wood felt under my hand. You know what I mean?"

Danny was intrigued, now, and as he asked questions about Tillie's experiences with her husband, she began to relax a little bit.

She used every bit of her creativity and imagination in her replies, trying to pique Danny's curiosity and lead to more questions.

Her only hope was to keep the young man interested until help arrived. What she would do if Honora never made it safety, or couldn't bring help, she wouldn't let herself think about.

33

Frustrated at not hearing from Ransom by morning, and feeling more like his old self, Slim decided to look for Tillie on his own.

He suspected she might have gone back to the park and feared she'd also suffered a misadventure. His mind filled with one awful scenario after another as he drove down the hill from his house, making his way to the park entrance.

Still a bit shaky, Slim forced himself to walk slowly along the damp path. He wouldn't be able to help Tillie if he fell again.

He didn't find any sign of her on the trails and had traipsed deeply into the misty trees when he caught sight of a bright flash of orange, similar to a cardigan Tillie often wore, and veered in that direction.

Getting closer, his stomach turned over as he recognized Tillie's silly safari hat and the tangerine sweater among the weeds in a grove of trees.

"Tillie!" he cried out.

With his heart pounding and a lump in his throat, he hurried as quickly as he could to her side and dropped down on one knee beside the still figure. When he saw blond hair spilling out from under the pith helmet, he realized this wasn't Tillie, after all.

Turning the woman over, he recognized the photos from the news reports; this was the missing Anniston girl!

He felt for a pulse, but couldn't tell if he was feeling the throbbing in his own fingers or the girl's faint heartbeat. Leaning close to her mouth, his cheek felt a weak rush of air through her bluish lips. Although unconscious and very pale except for the dark bruise on her temple, she was still breathing.

Frantic, Slim pulled out his phone and called for help.

"Yes, I'm sure it's the Anniston girl. She's in a bad way and needs an ambulance in a hurry," he urged the emergency operator.

Slim took off his jacket and covered Honora with it. Sitting beside her on the damp earth, he rubbed her hand and stroked her brow, gestures he knew comforted himself more than the unconscious girl. Ears straining for the welcoming sound of sirens, he rocked back and forth, his mind full of questions.

What the heck was this girl doing in Tillie's clothes? Where was Tillie?

*

Tillie had been telling stories, real and imagined, throughout the long night. The two had dozed off a few times in the darkness only to pick up where she left off each time she woke.

Danny had become almost docile during her ramblings, but Tillie remained ever alert for a change in his volatile moods.

She was beginning to feel like Scheherazade

when Danny suddenly grew restless during an account of her trip to Egypt. He'd picked up the piece of rope lying at his feet and was fiddling with it distractedly, when he suddenly jerked his head and jumped up from the chair, glaring.

"Hey! You let her go!" he shouted, fist clenched. "Honora's mine. Where is she?"

"I, uh, I don't know. Why don't you sit down and I'll finish telling you about the wonderful carvings we found in the king's burial chamber?"

Furious now, Danny whipped the coils of rope at Tillie, hitting her across the shoulder and knocking her off balance. She allowed herself to fall sideways onto the cot and rolled off onto the floor, stalling for time.

Danny kicked her once, then kicked the chair he'd been sitting on, and threw the rope across the room.

He crouched beside Tillie and jerked her head up by her braid, but she kept her eyes closed and he let her flop back onto the floor.

Pacing around the cramped space, he became more incoherent as he stomped around kicking out at whatever crossed his path; whether inanimate objects or Tillie's curled up form.

She ignored the cold seeping from the concrete into her aching body, focused on the many blessings in her long life and prepared to meet her Lord. It seemed He had no more work for her to do in this world, after all.

*

At the hospital, Slim was standing outside the Intensive Care room looking through the observation window at Honora's parents who were standing beside the bed of their unconscious daughter. He watched Mr. Anniston put his arm around his wife's shoulders as she leaned into him, sobbing with a mixture of relief and worry.

Slim wished his discovery of their child had been more joyful, but their ordeal wasn't over, according to the doctor. Tests were still being performed to uncover the reason for Honora's coma. There was no way to know what the poor girl had been through in the days of her capture or during her escape.

Because of the hat and sweater Honora was wearing when he found her, Slim was sure Tillie had something to do with the girl's release. He was frantic to know where his dear friend was and if she was okay. He prayed she was in better shape than Honora.

John Ransom stepped up to the observation window beside Slim.

"How's she doing?" he asked, nodding at Honora.

Slim told Ransom what he knew and walked with him into the family chapel around the corner from the ICU. They sat in a pew and Ransom pulled out his notepad.

"You found her in the park, is that right?" he asked.

"Yeah. When I didn't hear anything from you, I got restless. I figured Tillie might have gone investigating back at the park. You know what she's like. I was looking for her, but I found that poor little gal, instead. She was wearing Tillie's safari hat and one of her favorite sweaters, so they had to have been together at some point."

"I'm sorry I didn't call you last night, Mr. Bottoms. I was following up on a lead after I went to her house. I wanted to see where it led before telling you about it."

"What lead? Do you know where she is?" Slim asked, leaning toward the shorter man.

"No. That's not what I meant."

"Then what?"

"Well, when I got to her house she wasn't home, obviously. But there was a little carved figure on her porch. I thought it might be another of her garden ornaments, until I saw how much it resembled Mrs. T."

"But, what does that mean?" Slim asked.

"Possibly, nothing. It could connect her disappearance with a recent dog killing, though, so

I wanted to check it out," Ransom said.

"That dog killing got anything to do with the Whipple kid?" Slim asked, getting a sinking feeling.

"Well, it might. That's what I wanted to look into."

"Come on, detective. You know Tillie and I were following that guy. This morning I remembered he was with me in the park before I took that tumble. What if he's the one who knocked me down? What if he's got Tillie?" Slim asked, becoming increasingly agitated. "We've gotta find that kid."

Slim started for the chapel door and Ransom caught up to him, putting a hand on his arm to detain him.

"I've got a couple of officers looking for Danny Whipple, right now. I've been trying to reach him or his mother, but no one's been home. I'm going to leave someone watching the house, and then I'm going to join the men searching the park. They are fanning out from the spot where you found the girl. If Mrs. T. is anywhere nearby, they'll find her."

"I'll come with you. I can't just sit around."

"I tell you what; when I was at her house, I heard her cat inside and it sounded hungry. If you have a key, you could go take care of her pets and just let the professionals handle the search," Ransom said, patting Slim on the shoulder.

Reluctantly, Slim left. He knew Tillie would want him to take care of Agatha and Edgar, but he was heartsick with worry.

After Slim left the hospital, Ransom returned to the observation window outside Honora's room.

He'd been so sure she was a victim of the Coastal Killer, when all along she'd been held right in the community. Calling off the local search might have resulted in the girl's death. It looked like it still could.

He mentally kicked himself for jumping to

316

conclusions and was determined not to make the same mistake with Mrs. T.

34

In the park, a handful of officers fanned out from the spot where Honora had been found, looking for anything which might lead them to her captor or to Tillie.

When a contingent of searchers reached the slough, they used long sticks to poke among the reeds, while others approached the abandoned development acreage.

*

Underground, Danny stopped his tantrum when he heard voices overhead.

He hurried up the ladder and quietly pulled the hatch cover closed, then dropped down beside Tillie, and rolled her to face him.

"Don't make a sound, old woman," he hissed, raising his fist in an unseen threat in the all-encompassing darkness.

318

Tillie grimaced, wiping his spittle off her face, and responded to the threat in his voice with a nod.

Buoyed by the sounds of possible rescue, she tried to gauge her chances of making herself heard through the inches of concrete, before Danny could make good on his threats. Screaming too soon could result in a beating without alerting those overhead, while if she waited too long, the opportunity might slip away. With the hatch firmly closed, she couldn't hear the searchers and would have to guess when they might be near enough.

*

One of the deputies noticed the maintenance bunkers scattered across the development and, leaving the main body of searchers behind, he began systematically testing the access hatches. Most were overgrown and had obviously not been opened in decades, but he tried them all, anyway, without success.

He was walking toward the last one when

his radio crackled, directing him to respond to an emergency across town.

He looked at the unchecked bunker and, deciding someone else would check it when the other searchers reached the area, he jogged back through the park to his cruiser.

He was more than a hundred yards away when she cried for help and he never heard Tillie's scream, nor the loud slap she received for her efforts.

35

Marjie Whipple had finally returned his voice mail message and Ransom drove over to her home to question her.

Mrs. Whipple sat tautly on the edge of her chair, clear across the room from where Detective Ransom rested on the sofa.

"Where is your son?" he asked.

"Why?" she asked, rubbing her fingers together in her lap.

"Look, Mrs. Whipple, I know all about your son's history," he said. "We've had a couple of recent incidents which seem to indicate your son could be involved. Do you know where he is, now? I need to ask him a few questions."

"That was a long time ago. Danny was just a little boy. Little boys sometimes take things. They don't know any better. Why are you bringing it up, now?"

"It's our job to follow up on any possible lead. We can't eliminate Danny without talking to him."

"He hasn't done anything wrong, so you are wasting your time," she said, pressing her lips firmly together.

"Maybe, but I do need to speak to your son. Please tell me where he is."

"I don't know. He's usually home around this time, but he wasn't here when I woke up today. I work nights, you know. So, I can't help you. Why don't you leave your number and I'll have Danny call you when he returns?" she suggested, standing up.

"Can you tell me where your son might go? He doesn't work, does he?" Ransom asked, making no move to leave.

"He certainly does work! He has a part-time job doing something with websites on his computer. I don't understand it, but he gets paid.

He's not lazy, you know. It's hard for young men to find work these days."

"And where does he go when he's not at his computer? Does he have any friends he might visit?" Ransom asked again.

"No, his friends don't live around here, but he has lots of them on-line," she said, sitting back down with a sigh.

Ransom raised his eyebrows, holding his pen above his notebook, and she shrugged and went on.

"He goes out to run errands for me sometimes," she said. "He likes to take long walks in the park. He's not one to spend all his time indoors, your know."

"Did you have any errands for him today?" Ransom asked.

"No. He probably went out for a walk. He should be home again before long, though."

"Well, then, why don't I take a look in his room while we wait," Ransom said, standing up and gesturing for Mrs. Whipple to lead the way.

*

When Slim arrived at Tillie's empty house, he unlocked the door and stepped inside, and was overcome by a wave of loneliness. What would he do if she wasn't found? If something had happened to her?

At their ages, Slim and Tillie were aware each new day was precious and the shadow of death loomed ever closer. As believers, they didn't fear death and they often talked about the days to come when they would say goodbye to this life. However, the prospect of going on without his dear companion pierced Slim's heart. He'd always assumed he would be the first to cross over and would be waiting for Tillie on the other side, along with their loved ones who had gone before.

Pulled from his reverie by Agatha climbing up his leg to get his attention, he picked her up, detached her claws from his trousers and walked into the kitchen.

"Where's your mama, Aggie?" he asked the cat while looking through the cupboards for her canned food.

Agatha meowed, mournfully.

"You miss her, too, don't you?" he said. "She has a lot of confidence in her friend, John Ransom, and he's promised to find her. So, we'll just pray she's right about him."

With food in her dish, the cat was no longer listening to Slim's monologue, so he left her and attended to the tortoise.

Slim settled Edgar in his freshened night terrarium and watched him move slowly toward his food. The normally inexpressive creature seemed to Slim to be worried about Tillie, too.

Slim looked around Tillie's tidy bedroom and breathed in the subtle scent of herbs and spices he always identified with his dear friend. A lump formed in his throat. He coughed and hurried out into the hallway.

Agatha, finally replete, wandered from the

kitchen and wound herself around his legs as he stood trying to think what he should do next.

Slim lifted the purring cat into his arms and carried her into the sitting room where he sat in Tillie's rocking chair.

Agatha proceeded to wash herself vigorously, until Slim pushed her off onto the floor.

"I'm not your bathtub, silly cat," he said, smiling as Agatha calmly resumed licking herself at his feet. Her stomach full, her worries evaporated, and all seemed to be well in the cat's world.

Slim longed for a similar sense of peace.

"Oh, Tillie, where are you?" he whispered, leaning back with his eyes closed.

*

Ransom opened the door and looked into Danny's room. Blackout curtains covering the windows blocked out the sunshine. He groped for the light switch and clicked it on, illuminating an unmade bed dominating the center of the large room whose walls were plastered with posters featuring video game characters.

A corner unit housing a computer, monitor, and printer seemed to be the place Whipple conducted his web-based job. This was flanked by bookcases displaying dozens of collectible miniatures interspersed with original wooden and clay sculptures.

A worktable cluttered with carving tools and pieces of wood was pushed against the far wall.

Ransom picked his way around piles of discarded clothing and approached the table, wrinkling his nose against the room's stale locker room odor.

Turning to the array of miniatures, he focused on Danny's handiwork, which displayed the progression of his skill from nearly formless lumps of clay to truly sophisticated carvings.

One of the carvings caught Ransom's eye. It vaguely resembled the transient who'd found Honora's backpack. Upon closer inspection he realized the statue's face featured a distinctive scar reminding Ransom of a homeless man whose body had been discovered floating in the slough a few years before. At the time, the man's death had been ruled accidental.

Ransom set the figure back on the shelf with a frown.

A cork board hanging above the worktable held photos and clippings torn from the local newspaper. A large poster advertised the prior June's Tillamook Dairy Parade and featured a photo of some of the dancers from the Twinkle Toes Dance Studio, including Honora Anniston. All the clippings were about this same dance group.

Ransom stepped into the doorway and called down.

"Mrs. Whipple, would you mind coming up here?"

In a few moments Danny's mother appeared at the top of the stairs.

"Can you explain why your son is so

interested in the Twinkle Toes Dance Studio?" he asked.

Mrs. Whipple looked at the bulletin board.

"Isn't that the sweetest thing?" she said, obviously pleased.

"What do you mean?" Ransom asked.

"That's one of the places where I work as a cleaner. It's just like my boy to show an interest in my work."

"I don't see clippings from any other businesses. Why only this one?"

"Well, Danny used to come with me when he was little and the dance studio was his favorite spot. He loved to look at the pictures of the dancers they have on the walls."

"Did he take an interest in any particular dancer?" Ransom asked.

"I don't think so. Why would he? He was just a little kid," she replied.

Ransom thanked her, took a few photos of the clipping collection and the carving of the man with the scar.

Making a last scan of the room, he noticed a can on the floor beneath Danny's work table and picked it up. It was a pressurized engine starter product.

Ransom read the ingredients and saw that it contained ether.

Why did the kid need engine starter in his bedroom?

"Mrs. Whipple," he asked. "Has your son ever been involved with drugs?"

Standing in the doorway, Mrs. Whipple looked outraged at the question.

"Of course not! Why would you ask that?"

"He's never been known to abuse spray cans or sniff glue? You know, huffing?"

"I've never even heard of that, and my son has nothing to do with drugs. I think you should go, now."

Ransom nodded and went out, taking the can with him.

If he wasn't using the fluid to get high, what had the Whipple kid used it for?

36

In the ICU, Honora's parents kept a hopeful vigil. Side by side in uncomfortable plastic chairs, clasping each other's hands, they whispered to each other, their eyes never leaving their daughter's face.

"Oh!" Mrs. Anniston gasped. "She blinked! Howard, did you see?"

"I missed it. But, remember what the nurse told us. Little twitches don't necessarily mean she's waking up."

"I suppose," Ruth slumped. "She will wake up, won't she?"

"It's in God's hands, now, dear."

Ruth nodded, sending up another in a steady stream of silent prayers.

When Honora went missing, Ruth thought the worst torture was not knowing where her daughter was, or what was happening to her, but this current torment was even worse. Surely, God would not restore Honora to them, only to snatch her out of their grasp at the last moment.

"Mom?" a soft voice rasped, and the Annistons jumped to their daughter's side, Howard's chair crashing over backwards.

"We're here, darling!" Ruth cried, clutching her daughter's hand.

"Thank you, Jesus!" Howard whispered, before going into the hall to get the nurse's attention.

*

When Ransom learned Honora was conscious, he hurried to the hospital.

"She's weak and a little disoriented," the doctor told him. "You can see her for a few minutes, but she's suffering from a head injury along with the other effects of her confinement. She may drift in and out for a while before becoming fully conscious."

"Thank you, doctor. I'll go easy," Ransom said and joined Honora's parents at her bedside.

"It's a miracle," Mrs. Anniston greeted him with a smile. "I just knew she was alive!"

"I guess you were wrong, after all, detective," Mr. Anniston said. "You wanted us to give up."

"I'm happy to be wrong in this case, sir, believe me," Ransom replied. "I'd like to ask your daughter a few questions, if she feels up to it," he said, addressing this last to Honora as a question.

She nodded and her mother helped her take a sip of water.

"My head's still all foggy, though," she said, sinking back into the pillows.

"Do you remember meeting an elderly lady? You were wearing some of her clothes when you were found."

Honora closed her eyes and seemed to drift off.

"She needs her sleep, detective," her mother

said.

Frustrated, Ransom turned to go when Honora opened her eyes and spoke.

"She saved me. Can I thank her?" she asked.

"Her name is Matilda Thistlethwaite, Honora, and she's missing. I hope you can help us find her," Ransom explained, excited to confirm his suspicions. "Where did you see her?"

"In the hole in the ground," Honora whispered before slipping away again.

When she didn't wake up right away, a nurse rushed in and checked her vitals.

"She's sleeping," the nurse reassured Honora's worried parents, then turned to Ransom.

"She will probably sleep for an hour of more. I'm afraid you'll have to come back to finish your questions later."

Ransom went out as the nurse was suggesting to Honora's parents this would be a good time to take a break for a meal and a bit of rest.

*

Ransom sent word to the men searching the park that Honora had encountered Tillie in some sort of underground chamber. He was on his way to join the search when his mobile phone rang.

"Is there any word about Tillie?" Slim barked the minute Ransom answered.

"I spoke briefly with the Anniston girl. She wasn't fully alert, but she said she met Mrs. T. in a hole in the ground. I'm just on my way to the park to join the searchers. I'll check back with you as soon as I know anything."

Ransom ended the call and, feeling a renewed sense of urgency, switched on his siren.

He hadn't been in the park long and was coordinating with his men near the entrance when Slim pulled into the parking area, climbed out of his car, and approached, moving stiffly, as though still feeling the effects of his recent fall.

"Mr. Bottoms, you can't be here. Let the professionals do our job," Ransom said.

"But, I can help. I know where Tillie and I ran into the Whipple kid, and where I found the missing girl, and all."

"I won't make you leave, but you must stay behind the searchers and keep well out of the way. If you interfere, I will have you escorted home and set a guard on you, or lock you up, if I have to."

37

Tillie moaned and pushed herself up. Hearing her, Danny whirled around with his arm raised as though to strike her again.

"If you are finished throwing your tantrum, young man, I'm getting up off this cold floor. It makes my joints ache," she said, using the ladder to steady herself.

After closing the hatch, Danny had removed his battery operated lantern from an inconspicuous makeshift cupboard in an alcove behind the ladder and turned it on. It threw the room and its occupants into sharp relief, making Tillie's situation seem even more frightening.

She had huddled on the floor for what seemed like hours before deciding to pull herself together and begin to use her wits. While conjugating the verbs of an ancient language to

338

calm her mind, she'd thought of a possible way to distract Danny. A tribal song and dance she'd learned in Peru decades before might be silly enough to intrigue this odd and unpredictable young man.

Tillie began to sing, softly, almost under her breath, just loudly enough to hopefully prick the boy's curiosity.

"What are you saying?" he barked. "Are you trying to put a spell on me, or something?"

Tillie sang louder and added movements to her performance.

"Stop that! Are you crazy?"

Tillie stopped the song and replied, "This is a song of the ancient peoples of Peru. Almost no one in the world uses this language. Only someone very clever can sing this song. The legend says it can bring special powers to the singer. Singing it and doing the dance of the shamans always calms me down. I've even gotten myself out of a couple of sticky situations simply by singing and dancing as the witch doctors taught me. Of course, I don't really believe in any old ancient magic."

Danny was silent a few moments before saying, "Teach it to me."

"Oh, I don't know...."

"Teach me. Now," he said, raising a threatening fist.

Tillie flinched, saying, "Well, if you insist. I'll teach it to you phonetically. You don't need to know what the words mean for the magic to work. Listen carefully, and repeat the syllables I sing."

Tillie sang short snatches of the tune, matching her movements to the rhythm for Danny to mimic.

He became so totally absorbed in the song and dance, it gave Tillie hope he'd actually fallen for her fib about witch doctors and special powers.

*

The search party, now joined by several additional officers, tramped over the park, covering territory already searched, but this time looking for a hole in the ground big enough to conceal Honora and Tillie.

Rocks were overturned and shrubs pushed aside in hopes of finding the entrance to an underground chamber.

One searcher came upon someone huddled in a niche under a bridge and called the detective over, but it was a transient sleeping off a bottle of cheap wine. Ransom had the man taken into the station to sober up and resumed the search.

The methodical investigators plodded on, with Slim, carefully twenty yards back, getting more frantic by the moment.

They were running out of areas to search, having reached the abandoned development on the edge of the woods. Ransom's hopes were fading. Had he misunderstood Honora's words? Or had she been delirious?

Walking near yet another concrete abutment, he thought he heard muffled singing.

"What the heck?"

The singing got louder when he rounded the wall and he saw what looked like a metal and concrete manhole cover. The edges were no longer embedded with dirt and it was clear of weeds.

His heart leapt. This could be the spot.

If it was, why did he hear singing? The words made no sense, but it was definitely human voices he heard and they seemed to be coming from beneath his feet.

Ransom gestured to his men to gather around, pulled out his weapon, and indicated for two of the men to open the hatch.

"This is the police! Come out with your hands up!" he called down and waited for a response.

The singing stopped, changing to murmured conversation before Tillie's round face appeared at the foot of the ladder, looking up.

"Is that you, John?" she asked, blinking. "Now, don't shoot. We're coming up."

She turned and spoke to someone behind

her, then stepped back.

Danny Whipple, looking ashamed and frightened, began to climb the ladder.

When he reached the top, Tillie followed, biting her lips to stifle a moan as she pulled herself up each rung.

When her head was above ground and Ransom got a good look at her bruised face, he gasped and rushed to help her out of the hole.

When she stood on the surface, Tillie saw Danny, in handcuffs, being marched away by two officers.

"Are you okay, Mrs. T.?" Ransom asked..

"Tillie!" Slim cried, pushing past Ransom and taking her into his arms.

Tillie leaned into Slim's embrace with a sigh, allowing herself to relax, at last.

"Here, sit down," Slim said, easing her onto the low wall surrounding the trapdoor.

"Can you tell me what happened?" Ransom asked, his face pale.

Tillie took a breath to compose herself. She fought back tears and her voice trembled as she told about finding Honora and getting captured.

"You should never have come out by yourself," Slim chastised her, stroking her hand.

"You're right, of course. But, if I hadn't, that poor girl might still be down there," she replied with a ghost of her usual mischievous smile.

"And if we hadn't come along, you might still be down there, too, or you both might be dead," Ransom said, then as an afterthought asked, "What in the world was all the singing about?"

"It's a long story and I'm a mess. I need to get cleaned up. Why don't you take me home to change and we can have cookies and tea while I tell you men all about it," she said, getting up.

When Tillie got to her feet, the pain in her side caused her to stagger and sit back down.

"Stay right there," Detective Ransom insisted. "I'm going to get an ambulance. We need to get you to the hospital."

"I'll be fine. I just got a stitch in my side," Tillie said.

"Now you just sit still like he said," Slim said. "You might be hurt. You need to be checked out by a doctor. I know you think you are Wonder Woman, but you aren't invulnerable."

"Wonder Woman? Pfft!" Tillie scoffed.

It was plain that her pride had once again gotten her into trouble. She began to tremble as the true peril of her ordeal washed over her. She wasn't sure she would be capable of walking out of the park, even if John and Slim allowed it, hurting as she was from chagrin and the pain in her side.

38

Tillie was examined in the ER and admitted. Along with numerous scrapes and contusions, she had two broken ribs.

Once settled in a room, she greeted Slim with a rueful smile.

"I know what you are going to say and you're right. I should not have gone investigating on my own."

"No, you shouldn't have, but I wasn't going to say, I told you so. I never kick a woman when she's down," Slim said, pulling the visitor's chair up to the bedside and sitting.

"Too bad Danny Whipple didn't share that philosophy. If he did, I wouldn't have these broken ribs."

"He kicked you?!" Slim said, rising from the chair as if bent on thrashing Whipple.

346

"Sit down, sit down," Tillie said, waving a hand. "We've just had a painful lesson in letting the authorities handle this sort of thing, remember?"

Slim sat down and grasped her hand.

"You had me really scared, old girl. I don't know how you could be so calm, stuck down in that hole with a crazy man."

"I'll confess to being less calm than I may have looked. Danny Whipple is a disturbed, unpredictable young man. It's thanks to God I was able to keep him distracted a bit after Honora got away."

"What were you two singing, anyway?"

"Just a catchy Dumi children's game from Peru, but I convinced poor Danny it might give him special powers and help him escape his due punishment. I don't think he meant to harm the girl, not really. He was simply deluded and thought he could make her love him. It's sad, really."

"Not as sad as it might have been, thanks to

you," Slim said, patting Tillie's hand.

The nurse brought in a flowering plant, set it on the bedside table and handed Tillie the card.

"How lovely!" Tillie exclaimed. "It's from the church family. Isn't that nice? I wonder who told them I'm here."

Slim took the card and read it, nodding.

"You know how fast news travels in a small town," he said. "Somebody in the church probably has a relative on the force or working here in the hospital."

Tillie shifted in the bed and winced.

"What's wrong?" Slim asked, leaning forward.

"Just a twinge, it's gone now. The doctor said I should be good as new in a couple of days. He was surprised I'm in such good shape for an old gal," she said, smiling.

Slim and Tillie were chatting when the nurse stepped into the room, again.

"You have another visitor, Mrs.

Thistlethwaite. Do you feel up to seeing Mrs. Whipple?"

"That boy's mother? What's she doing here?" Slim asked, standing up.

"It's all right. Slim, why don't you go have a cup of coffee or something while I have a visit with Marjie Whipple," Tillie said, gesturing to the nurse to show her in.

Danny's mother, looking even more mouse-like than usual, sidled into the room avoiding Slim's glare as he walked out, and stopped at the foot of the bed.

"Come in, Marjie. Sit down," Tillie said. "It's nice of you to visit. Many people just hate hospitals."

"I came to apologize for my boy," Mrs. Whipple said, looking at the floor.

"Please sit down beside me, so we can talk," Tillie said.

Mrs. Whipple hesitated, then walked up and stood behind the chair, clutching its back with white-knuckled fingers.

"Do sit down, so I don't have to tilt my head up, dear," Tillie said.

Mrs. Whipple released her grasp to slide around and perch stiffly on the edge of the chair.

"My Danny is a good boy. He didn't mean any harm."

"I believe you are right, Marjie. However, although he didn't mean harm, harm was the result of his actions. Honora and the Annistons may never recover from her ordeal. My friend, Mr. Bottoms, might have been killed or permanently damaged when Danny hit him with a rock, and I'm in this bed with broken ribs because of the harm your son did."

Mrs. Whipple flushed and started to get up, but Tillie gestured for her to remain.

"I understand that your son doesn't think through how his actions affect other people. He isn't capable. But he can't be allowed to do these things ever again. I don't blame you for trying to protect him. I'm sorry this is as much a tragedy for you as it is for any of us."

Mrs. Whipple wiped a tear from her cheek and sniffed.

"There's a box of tissues here beside the bed," Tillie offered.

Mrs. Whipple used a tissue and regained her composure.

"Well, I just felt I had to come. Thank you for seeing me," she said and walked to the door.

"Thank you for coming," Tillie called as the woman walked out into the corridor.

Tillie sank back into the pillows, grimacing a bit from the pain. She closed her eyes and prayed silently for the Whipple and Anniston families.

When Slim returned to the room he found Tillie sound asleep. He was sitting beside her bed reading his new mystery novel when Olivette Vernon tiptoed in.

"Oh, is she sleeping? I'll come back later," she whispered.

Tillie's eyes popped open and she blinked, looking disoriented, then, seeing Olivette, she smiled.

"Olivette! How nice to see you. Come in," she said.

Slim stood for Olivette to take his place on the visitor's chair.

"I didn't mean to bother you, Tillie," Olivette said. "I just wanted to see for myself that you are all right. I can come back, later."

"Nonsense! Sit down. Sit down," Tillie said. "Slim you look exhausted. Why don't you go home and get some rest? I'm feeling much better after my nap. In fact, from the looks of you, you probably feel worse than I do. Shall I call the nurse to get you a bed?"

"That won't be necessary. I had my fill of hospital beds for a good while. I'll go home, but you call if you need anything, you hear?"

Slim leaned down and planted a gentle kiss on Tillie's forehead, smiled at Olivette, and left.

"Now then, fill me in on all the rumors flying around," Tillie said. "I want to know what misinformation is being spread around before I can get out of here and set everyone right."

39

Tillie finished the bland cream of wheat on her breakfast tray and pushed the tray aside. She attempted to get up for a trip to the bathroom, but found it too painful.

She rested back on the pillows and buzzed for a nurse.

"Good morning," said a cheerful young man dressed in scrubs.

Male nurses still surprised Tillie. Some changes of modern life were harder to adjust to than others and her ingrained expectation was for nurses to be female and doctors male. She didn't disapprove of the expanded roles, but usually required a moment to overcome her initial confusion.

"How can I help this morning?" the nurse asked.

"I need to use the bathroom, but I'm having a bit of trouble getting off the bed."

"Here you go," he said, lowering her bed and helping her sit up so she was able to swivel around and put her feet on the floor.

Bending over was painful and Tillie felt with her feet for her slippers.

The nurse, wearing a badge with the name "Thom" on it, retrieved the fuzzy slippers and put them on for her.

"Thank you," Tillie said, getting slowly to her feet. She swayed and put out a hand.

Thom steadied her and helped her walk across to the bathroom.

"I've got it from here, thank you, Thom," she said, going into the room and closing the door.

Thom was waiting for her when she emerged and Tillie found herself grateful for his support on the return trip to the bed.

She was alarmed and annoyed at her fragility. She had expected to wake up this morning fit as a fiddle and ready to go home. It seemed she had overestimated herself, once again.

Tillie was back in bed, washed and with her hair freshly braided, when in mid-morning her friend Opal peered through her door.

"Are you feeling up to a visitor?" she asked when Tillie looked up from the book she was reading.

"Opal! What a nice surprise. Come in, come in!"

"Well, you look okay," Opal said. "What did that crazy boy do to you, anyway?"

"Broke a couple of ribs, but I'll soon be good as new," Tillie said.

Opal pulled up the visitor's chair and sat.

"I just can't hardly believe my premonition was so accurate. I'm sure sorry I got you into this," she said.

"How do you figure that?" Tillie asked.

"If I hadn't told you about little Danny being our magpie, you would never have been prowling around, following him into danger. I owe Slim an apology, too, although strictly speaking, he's your fault."

Slim walked into the room, hearing the last few words.

"So, I'm Tillie's fault, eh? What'd I do now?" he asked, grinning,

He walked up to Tillie's bed and kissed her on the cheek while stroking her hair.

"How you feeling this morning?" he asked, sitting on the foot of her bed, then turned to Opal.

"Well, fess up. I heard what you said," he said.

"I was saying how bad I feel about getting you two into this mess with my old memories," Opal said.

"But, she thinks getting you into it can be laid at my feet," Tillie explained. "Of course, she's absolutely right."

"So you want all the credit, eh?" Slim asked Opal.

"Credit? Blame is more like it," she replied.

"I don't think the Annistons look at it quite that way," Slim said. "If you hadn't pointed us on the trail, their little girl might still be underground with that lunatic boy, or worse. We ran into a little trouble on the way to saving the day, but that's all down to Whipple, not you."

Opal, her forehead wrinkled in thought, was silent for a few moments before nodding with a huge smile.

"I never looked at it that way. I did help, didn't I? How about that?" she said. "I take back the apology, Tillie. Guess I'll be going. I'll drop by a basket of eggs and some honey and veg just as soon as you are home."

She patted Tillie's hand and turned to go, pausing at the door to ask, "When are you getting out of this joint, anyway?"

"Good question. The doctor hasn't come by, yet. I'm going to suggest he let me go home today," Tillie said.

Opal nodded and, with a wave, disappeared down the corridor.

"You made that woman's day, Slim," she said.

"What do you mean?"

"Opal may seem rough and ready, but she's one of the most tender-hearted people I know. She was agonizing over being responsible for our injuries. You lifted a huge burden off her shoulders and set her mind at rest."

"Glad to oblige," he mock bowed, doffing an imaginary hat.

Tillie's physician came by and remained unmoved by Tillie's pleas to be released.

"At least one more day of observation is called for at your age, Mrs. Thistlethwaite, so you can just relax and enjoy our hospitality. If no complications come up in the next twenty-four hours, and if you behave yourself, I might discharge you tomorrow," he said, going out.

"Oh dear," Tillie sighed.

"Now, don't fret," Slim said. "The doctor knows what he's doing. One more day of rest and relaxation will do you good. I'm looking after the critters, never fear."

"I appreciate that."

"Edgar's not much bother, but how you keep that feline fed is beyond me. She always thinks she's starving."

Tillie chuckled and flinched away from the pain in her side. Perhaps she wasn't quite ready to return home, after all.

Slim stayed to eat lunch with her, then had to leave, but Tillie was kept from boredom by frequent visits from her many friends. Classmates from her various classes, and her own yoga students, brought balloons, cards, and flowers giving her hospital room a festive air.

In a quiet moment, Tillie selected a chocolate truffle from a gift box and popped it into her mouth with a muffled, "Yum."

Relaxing into her pillows, sleepy from pain

medication, Tillie sighed in utter contentment and silently thanked God for her blessed life.

40

"**Ransom**," the detective responded when the phone on his desk rang.

"Hello, John, I mean Detective Ransom," Harmony Billings, at her desk in LA, replied.

"Harmony! It's good to hear from you. What's up?" Ransom asked.

"I'm just wrapping up a few things for the District Attorney's case against our trucker. When I called to speak with our witness in Medford, I was told she had already discharged herself and left no forwarding address."

"That's too bad. Will they be able to convict without her testimony?"

"We've got his confession and the bodies of his other victims, but he hasn't agreed to a plea deal, yet, and Hope Masterson's witness testimony is important."

"How can I help you?"

"One of the nurses in Medford said Masterson mentioned she wanted to spend a few weeks lying on a beach. I've got my people checking the California beach towns, but I thought you could put out some feelers along the Oregon coast. I know it's not your problem, but we're stretched kind of thin here."

"I'm happy to help. Your guy had nothing to do with our girl's disappearance, thankfully, but many of his victims were from our neck of the woods."

"Thanks. I wondered why we couldn't get him to own up to taking your girl. When we offered to take the death penalty off the table if he'd tell us where he dumped the bodies, he admitted to his other victims, but he wouldn't budge on the Anniston girl."

"I'm sorry we confused things by thinking he was our perp, too."

"Don't be sorry. That was good police work.

I'm just glad everything worked out."

"Me, too," Ransom said.

There was an awkward pause before they both spoke at the same time, saying, "It was good to work with you."

John laughed before saying, "I hope we can get together again sometime."

"I'd like that," Harmony said.

Sergeant Forester entered Ransom's office with some forms for him to sign and Ransom reluctantly ended the call.

"FBI?" Forester asked.

"Just wrapping things up. The Coastal Killer has confessed and they've located all his victims. He's going away for a long time."

"So's our guy. At least, he'll be locked up with the other criminally insane types for the foreseeable future and things can get back to normal around here."

On his way out of the office, Forester picked up the empty cinnamon roll container from the top of the file cabinet and turned back.

"Say, don't you think we need to debrief Mrs. T. again?"

*

Marjie Whipple sidled into the visitors' room, slid onto a plastic chair facing the doorway, and waited for her son to appear.

When he came into the room in shackles between two guards, her heart twisted in anguish and she began to get up to go to him.

One of the guards motioned for her to sit down.

"No physical contact, ma'am."

She nodded with tears filling her eyes. A single drop slipped over her lower lid and she swept it away with a trembling finger.

The guards fastened Danny to his side of the table and stepped back, but remained in the room.

"Hello, son. How are you doing?"

Danny sat with his head down, mumbling and twisting his hands within cuffs.

"Danny? It's mommy, dear. Please look at me."

Lifting his head, Danny focused on his mother and smiled, dreamily.

"Hi, Mom," he said, before letting his head drop to his chest.

The brief look into his eyes showed the effects of the drugs he'd been given and Marjie recoiled.

Turning to the guards, she protested.

"What are they giving my son? He's out of his head on drugs!"

"You will need to speak with the doctor, ma'am," one of the men responded, while the other stood impassively.

Marjie pulled herself together, biting her lips.

"Danny, dear. I can see you need to rest, now. Mommy is going to talk to the doctor, but I'll be back to see you again when you feel a little better. Remember, Mommy loves you."

The guards unhooked his bindings and prepared to take Danny back to his cell. Before they left the room, Marjie asked where to find the doctor.

After making her way through several levels of bureaucratic delays, Marjie managed to make her way into the office of the doctor treating her son.

"Please be seated, Mrs. Whipple," the doctor said. "I'll be happy to tell you anything I can about your son's situation here."

"I want to know why he's been so heavily medicated. He can scarcely speak."

"I'm afraid our protocols require a certain regimen of medication for all new admissions. It ensures a smoother transition, especially for the sort of violent offenders we handle. The drugs are gradually reduced until the inmate can be evaluated."

"But, my son wasn't violent when he was arrested! He's not a bad boy. He was confused, but he didn't mean to hurt that girl. Can't you take him off the medication?"

"In the prescribed time, certainly. Your son is accused of kidnapping and several counts of inflicting grievous bodily harm on more than one individual. Until we determine the level of medication needed for the long-term, we must consider him at risk for violence. Perhaps it would be better if you were to leave now, and come back after he's been evaluated. I will leave instructions for you to be notified when your son is ready to receive another visit."

"But, but..," she protested.

"Thank you for stopping by. Rest assured your son is in good hands," the doctor said while ushering Mrs. Whipple out of his office. "Give my secretary your number where we can call you. You should hear from us in a week or two. Goodbye."

The doctor disappeared behind his closed office door, leaving Marjie dazed.

She saw the secretary holding out her hand

as if waiting for Marjie's business card. Flustered, Marjie pulled an empty envelope from her handbag and scribbled her name and phone number on it before giving it to the secretary.

Confused and upset, Marjie slumped down in one of the visitors' chairs rather than leaving immediately.

The secretary picked up the phone and said a few words and soon a security guard appeared and escorted Marjie out of the facility.

In the parking lot, she sat numbly behind the wheel of her sedan before starting the car and driving home to her empty house where she made herself a cup of tea and tried to think. She couldn't stand by while they treated her Danny like a dangerous criminal.

Remembering the kindness Tillie had shone her, Marjie pulled out the phone book and looked up her number.

41

"**Home** at last," Tillie sighed, dropping her handbag on the table in the foyer.

"Now, you come in here and put your feet up," Slim said, ushering her into the parlor.

"Thank you for bringing me home," Tillie said, easing down into her favorite rocking chair.

"Well, sure. I'm not about to leave my best friend stranded at the hospital, not like someone I could mention," he said, teasing.

"I am sorry about that, you know. I believe I have been punished enough for that particular lapse, don't you?"

Slim leaned over and kissed her cheek.

"What can I do for you, now? Is there anything you need before I go?" he asked.

"Well, since you asked…I'd love a cup of tea. If you have time, that is. I know you have a board meeting at church to get to."

"It won't matter if I miss the first few minutes. Those board meetings tend to make one bored, pretty quick. I'll get your tea."

Slim went into the kitchen and Tillie looked around her cozy room with satisfaction. It was good to be home.

Becoming aware of the muffled trill of her phone, Tillie made a sour face and pushed herself out of her comfy perch to answer it.

"Don't hang up! I'm coming," she addressed the unknown caller.

She hated to run for a phone call and have the caller hang up just as she answered. It frustrated her not to know who might have called.

"Hello!" she said, snatching up the phone and plopping into the nearest chair.

When no one spoke, she was about to hang up when she heard a voice.

"Hello. Mrs. Thistlethwaite?"

"Yes, who is this?"

"Marjie Whipple."

Tillie's eyebrows rose in surprise and for a moment she was speechless.

"Are you still there?" Marjie asked.

"Yes, yes. What can I do for you, Mrs. Whipple?" she asked, genuinely curious.

Marjie began haltingly, at first, then rapidly poured out her anguishing experience at the correctional department mental health facility. When she finished her story she was sobbing.

"Oh, dear, Marjie. No wonder you are upset," Tillie said. "But what do you think I can do to help?"

"You know my Danny. I know he hurt you, but you were able to talk to him and help him give himself up. I thought maybe you could explain to the people that he's not dangerous and violent. They don't need to drug him and chain him up like an animal!"

"Now, now. Take a deep breath and try to calm down. I happen to agree with you. Danny can't be allowed to hurt anyone else, whether from confusion or delusion, he needs to be in a locked facility where he can get help. That being said, he shouldn't be subject to heavy drugs and severe treatment."

"That's what I think, too!" Marjie said.

"I don't know what good it will do, but I will speak with my friend, Detective Ransom, and see if he can influence the facility to go easier on your son. I'm afraid there is nothing else I can do."

"Thank you, so much. You've given me hope. Thank you, thank you," Marjie said.

"I will let you know if John Ransom thinks he can help. In the meantime, I'll be praying for you and your son. Try not to worry. Good-bye."

Tillie did as she'd promised, saying a fervent prayer for the Whipples before picking up the phone and calling John.

She was just sitting down again when Slim returned with her tea, and a slightly stale date bar he'd discovered in her cookie jar.

"What are you doing? You are supposed to take it easy, remember?"

"I had to answer my phone. I left it in my bag. But, no worries. I've got it here beside me, now."

"Who called?" Slim asked.

"Just a friend," Tillie said.

She didn't think Slim would take too kindly to the idea of Mrs. Whipple asking favors, under the circumstances.

Slim frowned at Tillie's unusual reticence, then shrugged, deciding she was probably just worn out from the drive home from the hospital.

"You keep that phone with you, now, and call me if you need anything, you hear?" he said.

Tillie nodded, then picked up her tea and took a sip.

"Ah, perfect!" she sighed. "Thank you, dear. You'd better go now or you'll miss the meeting."

Slim looked at his watch and nodded.

"See you later!" he said and left.

Tillie set her cup down just before Agatha hopped into her lap, then she leaned back with her eyes closed to savor the sensation of being home, at last.

*

"That woman is really something!" he said, putting his phone down as Sergeant Forester walked into his office.

"Who?" Forester asked.

"Mrs. T. Who else? She just now called to ask me to advocate for special treatment for the Whipple kid."

"I don't blame her. Treatment in a mental hospital isn't enough for a kidnapper, and you saw the damage he did to Mrs. T, too. Does she want him sent to a Super Max prison for life or is she asking for the death penalty?"

"You misunderstand," Ransom said. "She wants the guy treated better."

"What!" Forester asked. "Why?"

"The kid's mother was over at the

correctional facility and found out her precious baby boy's all drugged up and in shackles. The woman had the nerve to call Mrs. T. and ask her for help."

"She asks one of his victims to help him? She's as loopy as her kid," Forester said.

"Apparently not, since she got what she wanted. Mrs. T. is convinced the kid isn't dangerous, as long as he's in a controlled environment. She wants me to try to get him off the heavy meds and restraints while the docs evaluate him," Ransom said.

"Are you going to do it?"

"I told her I would see what I can do. Those head-shrinkers don't take much notice of us, though. I can't tell them what to do."

Shaking his head, Forester left the office as Ransom reached for his telephone to call Danny's doctor.

42

Hope Masterson stepped down off the bus, looked around to get her bearings, and strode out of the Bannoch bus station following the signs pointing her toward the beach.

With her duffel bag slung over her good shoulder, a cast on her left wrist, and fading bruises on her face, the tall redhead looked like a soldier returning from battle. Even the huge smile when she caught sight of the ocean reflected the joy of a homecoming.

Hope closed her eyes and lifted her face into the sea breeze, savoring the salty tang and the fishy aroma, then crossed the highway to the boardwalk beach access.

It was a rare sunny late spring day on the Oregon Coast and the warm sand was dotted with people.

Hope dropped her bag at the edge of a dune, pulled off her shoes and socks and padded down to the hard packed sand near the surf where she stood staring out across the water and enjoying the sensation of the icy tide teasing at her bare toes.

A piece of driftwood sailed overhead, hitting the water nearby, and a large black lab splashed into the surf after it, spraying water in all directions.

"I'm sorry. I hope Texaco didn't get you too wet," a tall man in his late forties said. "It's my fault. I shouldn't have thrown the stick so close to you."

"No harm done," Hope shrugged. "I expected to get wet. It's a beach, after all."

"I'm Scott Davidson. Are you new in town?" he asked.

"Yeah. I just got off the bus," she said. "Hope Masterson."

"You arrived on a good day, Hope. It's been stormy all week, but the clouds parted this morning and the forecast is for at least a week of warmth and sunshine…and wind, of course. We get few breaks from the sea breeze."

The dog ran up with the stick and dropped it at Scott's feet, grinning expectantly.

"Nice dog. You said his name's Texaco? There must be a story behind that," Hope said.

"Yes. He was found as a puppy, abandoned in an old gas station. The name was my wife's idea, but he seems happy with it," Scott said, rubbing the dog's head.

Hope picked up the stick and tossed it into the surf, flinching slightly from a stab of pain in her shoulder.

"How did you hurt your arm?" Scott asked as the dog chased off. "If you don't mind my asking."

"I had a run-in with a bad guy down in California, but that's behind me and I'm not looking back," she said. "You're a local, right? Can you point me to a good place to stay for a couple of days?"

"Sure. I'm the pastor of the Bannoch Community Fellowship church and my wife runs a property management agency, so we are pretty familiar with the area. And, coincidentally, my sister and her husband have a cozy little Bed and Breakfast on the edge of town. It's within walking distance to downtown and has an ocean view, if that sounds like it would work for you."

"It might. Expensive?"

"I don't think so. I could drive you up there, so you can check it out. No obligation, of course. If it doesn't suit you, I'll bring you back here, or take you to one of the motels," Scott offered.

Hope gazed out at the sea and Scott busied himself throwing the stick for Texaco while she considered his proposition.

The bus ride from Medford to the coast had given Hope time to reflect on her life. She'd been walking a pretty independent path since leaving the military; not getting too close to anyone or putting down roots. For some reason, this preacher's suggestion appealed to her. Maybe it was time for her to find a place to call home. It wouldn't hurt to see if this seaside community might be a good spot to start.

"Thanks," she said, shaking Scott's hand. "I'll grab my kit and we can see what your sister's cozy B&B has to offer."

43

Three days after being released from the hospital, Tillie was sitting in her rocking chair enjoying the late spring sunshine pouring in through the living room window.

Edgar was in his playpen and Agatha was purring on Tillie's lap. The cat had been very clingy since Tillie's hospitalization.

The doorbell rang and Tillie called out, "Come on in, it's open!"

Slim stepped into the parlor.

"I see why you couldn't come to the door. Cat's got you pinned down, again."

"She acts as if she's afraid I'll abandon her. Didn't you feed the poor thing while I was gone?"

"Sure, but it's never enough for that one. Talk about high maintenance."

"There's coffee in the kitchen, if you want

some. You'll have to help yourself."

"I'll just do that," Slim responded and walked into the kitchen.

"That's the emptiest I've ever seen your kitchen, Tillie," he said, when he returned with his coffee. "There's not even a ghost of your good baking."

"The doctor told me to take it easy, so I have been."

"You listen to those doctors for much longer and they will have you living in Golden Memories with the other old codgers," Slim said, only half teasing.

Tillie chuckled and said, "I've been thinking the same thing. Tomorrow I'm getting back on track. I've got a yoga class to teach."

"Can you do that with broken ribs?" Slim asked, thinking he shouldn't have goaded Tillie. "You don't want to overdo it."

"Oh, I won't. I've drafted Olivette as my assistant. I'll give the instructions, but she will perform any of the positions I can't handle. She's younger than I am, too, so maybe she will take over from me when I move on past Ripe and Ready and become all Squishy and Silly."

"I heard the Whipple boy is probably going to be found unfit for trial, so he'll go to a secure mental facility. How do you feel about him dodging prison?"

"That boy's mind is enough of a prison. I'm not looking for revenge. My ribs are healing, but I wonder if he will ever be right in his mind."

"I ran into Howard Anniston in the post office yesterday. He said his girl is out of the hospital. He and his missus probably won't be as forgiving as you are."

"How is Honora doing after her ordeal?" Tillie asked.

"Her dad said she's healing quickly, physically, but he's worried about her emotional health. He's afraid she might come down with Post Traumatic Stress, so they are getting her in to see a counselor."

"It would be a miracle if she didn't have some psychological after-effects from her captivity. I've been sitting here thinking I should drop in on her," Tillie said.

She brushed Agatha off and stood up.

"There's no time like the present. Will you give me a lift?" she asked.

"Now? Are you sure you're up to it?"

"Of course. I'll just call to be sure she's up to a little company."

*

Slim escorted Tillie to the Anniston's door and pressed the bell.

Waiting on the doorstep, Tillie began to wonder if she was doing the right thing. Seeing her again could bring the horror of Honora's experiences flooding back.

Tillie turned to Slim to suggest that they leave just as the door was opened.

"Hello, Mrs. Thistlethwaite, Slim. Come on

in," Howard Anniston said, opening the door for his guests to enter.

"Thank you for seeing us, Mr. Anniston. I hope we aren't intruding. Your family has been through so much, lately. I wouldn't want to make things more difficult for you," Tillie said.

Hearing Tillie sounding so uncharacteristically diffident, Slim shot her a questioning look.

Howard ushered them into the family room, where his wife and daughter were waiting.

As soon as Tillie entered the room, Honora jumped up and enfolded her in an enthusiastic and rather painful hug.

"My hero!" she cried, stepping back and smiling.

Tillie was thrown off balance, both physically and emotionally, by Honora's greeting.

Slim put a steadying hand on her back while extending his other hand to Honora in greeting.

"Thanks for letting us drop in," he said. "We

wanted to see how you are doing after all the turmoil."

Ruth gestured for her guests to sit and offered them drinks.

"Nothing for me, thanks," Tillie said when she was settled on the sofa between Slim and Honora. "We don't want to be a bother, but I needed to see our girl, just to know she's okay."

"You aren't a bother," Honora said. "I've been wanting to see you. I even asked Dad to take me to your place, but he didn't think I should go out, yet, even though my bruises and scabs are mostly gone."

"You are looking remarkably recovered," Tillie said. "I didn't expect to find you so well. You were in pretty rough shape when I saw you last."

"Omigosh, I sure was! I thought I was going to die in that hole. I'll bet I would have, too, if you hadn't saved me," Honora said, giving her rescuer another painful squeeze. "How ever did you find me, anyway?"

"Tillie took against that Whipple boy the minute she saw him. She's got amazing intuition," Slim said. "I couldn't see it, at first, but then, neither did the police."

"No. They had the wrong end of the stick right from the start," Howard said.

"They thought Honora had run off with some boy," Ruth said, shaking her head.

"Tillie tried to get them to look at Whipple, but they were convinced that serial killer had got to her," Slim said with a nervous glance at Honora.

"No need to talk about that, now. She's safe and sound and in no more danger," Tillie said, patting Honora's hand.

"I don't mind talking about it, actually. Daddy thinks I'm suffering from repressed PTSD, or something, but I'm just glad it's all over. I mean, it was horrible and scary and all, but what are the odds of anything like that ever happening to me in the future? Stuff like that only happens once in a lifetime, right?"

"Right. That's a remarkably mature and healthy attitude," Tillie said, feeling reassured. "So, what are your plans? You missed a bit of schoolwork. How are you going to catch up?"

"Daddy wants me to do home school from now on, but I'm eager to get back to my classes. I'm sure the teachers will give me time to do my makeup work."

"Heck, yeah. Under the circumstances, I'd imagine they will allow even more time than usual," Slim offered, then turned to Howard, saying, "You can't keep her home from the world and all her friends, you know."

"It's such a dangerous world, though," Ruth said. "If anything else should happen to Honora, I don't think we could survive."

"Say, Ruth, I think I will take you up on that offer of a cup of tea. Let's go into the kitchen and I'll help. You want tea, too, don't you, Slim?" Tillie said with a nudge.

She tried to get up from the soft sofa, but was

having trouble reaching the floor with her short legs, so Slim gave her a boost and, without waiting for her hostess, she bustled into the kitchen.

Ruth had no option, but to follow.

Once they were alone, Tillie said, "I know it is not my business, Ruth, but I'm going to play the Wisdom of Age card and offer you some unsolicited advice."

"What do you mean?" Ruth said while filling the kettle.

"Out there, you said you and Howard want to keep your daughter safely at home, protected from the dangerous world, because you couldn't bear it if something else happened to her, right?"

"Yes. You would feel the same if it were your child."

"I would, and I would be just as wrong to act on those feelings as you will be," Tillie said.

Ruth frowned as Tillie continued.

"The parents' duty is to take care of their children while raising them up to be able to take

390

care of themselves. We are to think of their needs above our own, don't you agree?"

Ruth nodded.

"So, whose need is being met by you swaddling your girl in bubble wrap against all dangers, real or imagined?"

Ruth looked chagrined as she said, "Ours, of course."

"Your husband is seeing imagined psychological damage, while you are picturing all the horrors the wide world has to offer, just like any parents in your situation, but you must set those feelings aside for Honora's sake. She's a strong girl to have weathered this recent storm. You've raised her well and she is more than capable of handling whatever is ahead, as long as she has your loving support. Besides, even if you tried to keep her locked away like a princess in a fairytale tower, you couldn't protect her from every possible harm."

As she spoke, Tillie's thoughts drifted back to her own child's sudden death. She would always wonder if she and Gerald could have protected Gordon from his hidden heart defect. She was grateful they'd had fifteen wonderful years with him, and that he'd been so full of life and laughter.

"You're right. This has been such a nightmare, it's thrown us off-kilter," Ruth said.

"Seems like you are getting your equilibrium back, just fine. Do you have any cookies to go with that tea?"

Ruth gave Tillie a quick, gentle hug and turned to get a package of Fig Newtons from the cupboard.

When they returned to the family room, Honora jumped up to take the tray from her mother and turned to Tillie.

"Maybe you can convince them to let me go," she said as she put the tray on the coffee table.

"Go where?" Tillie asked, resuming her seat beside Slim and looking at the others for an explanation.

"New York, of all places," Howard

responded. "It's out of the question."

"But, they want me to come! This is my big chance!" Honora cried.

"I think you should explain, dear," Tillie said.

"Well, you know how there were all those news stories about what happened?" Honora asked.

Tillie nodded.

"The New York Dance Academy director saw how I was a dancer and felt sorry for me or something. Anyway, they sent me an invitation to attend their summer dance lab. It's a huge honor and if I do well, they might take me on as an apprentice dancer. Wouldn't that be great? It's a chance to make something super out of this whole mad experience. You agree, don't you?" Honora asked.

"It doesn't matter what Mrs. Thistlethwaite thinks, child. Your mother and I forbid it."

"But it does matter what she thinks! She

saved my life! Some people think that means I belong to her, now," Honora said, looking triumphant.

"I'm afraid we aren't in a culture with that particular custom, dear," Tillie said.

Howard crossed his arms, looking smug as he nodded his approval.

"However," Tillie went on, "for what it's worth, I think it might be an excellent opportunity for you. It's only a month or so in the summer, right? As long as you're chaperoned and your doctors approve, I can't see any problem."

Howard began to rise and Ruth forestalled him with her hand on his arm.

"I hadn't thought about the possibility of a chaperone," she said. "I haven't been to New York since my college days. Spending a few weeks in the Big Apple with my daughter sounds like fun."

"Do you mean it?" Honora asked, jumping up and hugging her mother.

"Only if your doctor says it's okay," Ruth

said. "And, if your dad can get along without us, of course."

Howard's face was red as he realized he'd been outflanked. He began to bluster, then saw the determination in his wife's eyes and slumped back as though deflated.

"I can certainly manage on my own for a few weeks, I suppose. I've used up my vacation during our ordeal or I would go with you. Perhaps I can still manage a long weekend to get you two settled in New York and see a few sites before I leave you to your mad adventure."

After all the recent sadness, the bright smile on his daughter's face, told Howard he was making the right decision.

"Thank you! Thank you!" she said, hugging her father and turning to Tillie. "And thank you for saving my life, again! I've got to go call Shantee and Samantha and tell them the news. This is so wild. They are going to freak."

Honora danced out of the room, leaving the

adults smiling after her.

"She seems to be recovering from her trauma, pretty well," Slim said to Howard. "She might not need those counseling sessions, after all."

"She's our little girl, Slim. We can't help worrying about her and trying to protect her, can we?" he replied.

"You are both wonderful parents. All anyone has to do is look at your daughter to see that," Tillie said.

She scooted to the edge of the sofa cushion to put her tea cup on the coffee table, saying, "Thanks so much for letting us drop in. I think we'd better be going."

They all stood and the Annistons walked with Tillie and Slim to the door, where they thanked them for coming.

Outside, Tillie stumbled on a crack in the sidewalk and Slim grabbed her arm to keep her from falling.

"Are you okay?" he asked.

"Of course," she said. "I am just a little tired, though, and all those enthusiastic hugs have my ribs aching. I'm ready to get back to my rocking chair."

"If you will let me, I'll stay and fix your dinner. You can just take it easy and send me home when you want to get to bed."

"That sounds delightful. Thank you," she said, getting into Slim's car.

*

John Ransom reviewed the Anniston/Whipple files, organizing the information and making additional notes where necessary, preparing the records for archiving as they would not be needed for a trial.

He looked at the three carved figures on his desk.

The lab found DNA evidence that they were Danny Whipple's work, but the boy had already confessed to leaving them at his victim's locations.

Ransom picked up the little dog figure.

Whipple had taken the dog to keep the Anniston girl company, part of his delusion. When the dog bit him, he'd killed it, but he had already given its owner the carved replacement. In the kid's twisted mind, swapping a carving for the real thing was a fair exchange.

Knowing the Dumont woman wouldn't want the carving, he dropped it into the evidence box and looked at the ballerina as Sergeant Forester walked in.

"Officer Willis is on the phone, again, sir. He's asking when he can return the dancer statue to the dance teacher. Apparently, she wants to keep it," he said.

"He can come and get it, now. We are done with it," Ransom said, handing the figure to Forester. "Leave it at the front desk for him to pick up."

Forester went out, leaving the last carving on the desk.

Ransom knew what to do with this one. It

would have a home on his desk, reminding him every day of the near-tragic miscalculation he'd made when he'd ignored Mrs. T.'s intuition.

It was a shame about Whipple. He had real talent. Not only was the carving an uncanny likeness of Mrs. T., but he'd somehow managed to capture her essence. In fact, he could almost smell the delectable aroma of yeast and spices every time he looked at it.

*

The sunlight had faded as the fog rolled in, so Slim got up and closed the parlor drapes, and then went back to his chair across from Tillie.

Tillie rocked gently in time to the classical music coming from the radio. Her eyes were closed and Agatha purring loudly on her lap.

"I guess I'd better get off home and let you rest," Slim said.

Tillie opened her eyes and smiled.

"That was a lovely dinner. I haven't had wieners and sauerkraut in ages."

"It's one of my specialties," Slim boasted.

"It was delicious. Thank you."

"I'm happy to help. You know that. Is there anything else I can do for you before I head out?"

"As a matter of fact, Edgar needs to be bedded down and it still sort of hurts my ribs to lift him up into the night terrarium."

"You got it," Slim said, getting up. He lifted the tortoise out of his playpen and carried him into Tillie's bedroom.

Tillie was standing in the hallway when Slim came out of her room.

"I haven't properly thanked you, have I?" she said.

"What for? It's no big deal to move Edgar for you."

"Not just for that, for everything. For helping to rescue me from my own foolishness; both recently and always. A true friend is to be treasured and I do treasure you. I don't tell you often enough."

Blushing, Slim cleared his throat before taking both Tillie's hands in his and looking down into her clear, blue eyes.

"I don't know as I'm such a treasure, but the feeling is mutual. I am proud to be your friend just as long as the Lord allows."

He leaned down, hugged her carefully, and brushed her cheek with a kiss.

"See you tomorrow," he said, going out with a wave.

Agatha wound around her legs, purring loudly, as Tillie stood with her hand on her cheek, feeling blessed and peaceful.

She locked the door and turned out the hall light before lifting the cat into her arms and carrying her into the bedroom. Dropping Agatha onto the bed, she sat to take off her shoes while the cat curled up on the colorful crazy quilt coverlet, a past birthday gift from Opal.

"It's been quite an exciting few weeks, hasn't it, Aggie? I wonder what the Lord has in store for us tomorrow?"

When she was ready for bed, Tillie pushed the cat over and slipped beneath the blankets.

"Old as I am, the world still holds surprises. Whatever lies ahead, I'd better get plenty of rest. I want to be ripe and ready for our next great adventure."

Acknowledgements

I would like to thank my hard-working proof-readers/editors, Donna and Neal.

Thanks to all my faithful fans for their support and kind reviews.

Special thanks to my fellow authors who so generously share experience, wisdom, encouragement, and welcome advice.

Made in the USA
San Bernardino, CA
11 November 2017